Forensic Art

THE TRICKSTER'S IMAGE

WITHDRAWN

THE CRIME SCENE CLUB: FACT AND FICTION

THE CRIME SCENE CLUB: FACT AND FICTION

Forensic Art
THE TRICKSTER'S IMAGE

Kenneth McIntosh

Mason Crest Publishers

THE TRICKSTER'S IMAGE: FORENSIC ART

MASON CREST PUBLISHERS INC.
370 Reed Road
Broomall, Pennsylvania 19008
(866)MCP-BOOK (toll free)
www.masoncrest.com

First Printing

9 8 7 6 5 4 3 2 1

ISBN 978-1-4222-0259-3 (series)
Library of Congress Cataloging-in-Publication Data

McIntosh, Kenneth, 1959–
   The trickster's image : forensic art / by Kenneth McIntosh.
      p. cm. — (Crime Scene Club ; case #3)
   Summary: Crime Scene Club member Ken Benally has not seen his mother in four years, so when it appears that she is involved in the theft of some valuable Native American artifacts from a local museum, he does not know what to think.
   Includes bibliographical references and index.
   ISBN 978-1-4222-0249-4   ISBN 978-1-4222-1452-7
   [1. Criminal investigation—Fiction. 2. Indians of North America—Arizona—Fiction. 3. Mothers—Fiction. 4. Interpersonal relations—Fiction. 5. Flagstaff (Ariz)—Fiction. 6. Mystery and detective stories.] I. Title.
   PZ7.M1858Tr 2009
   [Fic]—dc22

                              2008023304

Design by MK Bassett-Harvey.
Produced by Harding House Publishing Service, Inc.
www.hardinghousepages.com
Cover design by MK Bassett-Harvey.
Cover and interior illustrations by Justin Miller.
Printed in Malaysia.

CONTENTS

INTRODUCTION

The sound of breaking glass. A scream. A shot. Then . . . silence. Blood, fingerprints, a bullet, a skull, fire debris, a hair, shoeprints—enter the wonderful world of forensic science. A world of searching to find clues, collecting that which others cannot see, testing to find answers to seemingly impossible questions, and testifying to juries so that justice will be served. A world where curiosity, love of a puzzle, and gathering information are basic. The books in this series will take you to this world.

The CSI Effect

The TV show *CSI: Crime Scene Investigator* became so widely popular that *CSI: Miami* and *CSI: NY* followed. This forensic interest spilled over into *Bones* (anthropology); *Crossing Jordan* and *Dr. G* (medical examiners); *New Detectives* and *Forensic Files*, which cover all the forensic disciplines. Almost every modern detective story now involves forensic science. Many fiction books are written, some by forensic scientists such as Kathy Reichs (anthropology) and Ken Goddard (criminalistics and crime scene), as well as textbooks such as *Criminalistics* by Richard Saferstein. Other crime fiction authors are Sir Arthur Conan Doyle (Sherlock Holmes), Thomas Harris (*Red Dragon*), Agatha Christie (Hercule Poirot) and Ellis Peters, whose hero is a monk, Cadfael, an ex-Crusader who solves crimes. The list goes on and on—and I encourage you to read them all!

The spotlight on forensic science has had good *and* bad effects, however. Because the books and TV shows are so enjoyable, the limits of science have been blurred to make the plots more interesting. Often when students are intrigued by the TV shows and want to learn more, they have a rude awakening. The crime scene investigators on TV do the work of many professionals, including police officers, medical examiners, forensic laboratory scientists, anthropologists, and entomologists, to mention just a few. And all this in addition to processing crime scenes! Fictional instruments give test results at warp speed, and crimes are solved in forty-two minutes. Because of the overwhelming popularity of these shows, juries now expect forensic evidence in every case.

The books in this series will take you to both old and new forensic sciences, perhaps tweaking your interest in a career. If so, take courses in chemistry, biology, math, English, public speaking, and drama. Get a summer job in a forensic laboratory, courthouse, law enforcement agency, or an archeological dig. Seek internships and summer jobs (even unpaid). Skills in microscopy, instrumentation, and logical thinking will help you. Curiosity is a definite plus. You must read and understand procedures; take good notes; calculate answers; and prepare solutions. Public speaking and/or drama courses will make you a better speaker and a better expert witness. The ability to write clear, understandable reports aimed at nonscientists is a must. Salaries vary across the country and from agency to agency. You will never get rich, but you will have a satisfying, interesting career.

So come with me into this wonderful world called forensic science. You will be intrigued and entertained. These books are awesome!

—Carla M. Noziglia MS, FAAFS

Chapter 1
STRANGE ENCOUNTERS

The moment I saw Coyote, I knew it would lead to bad luck. I couldn't even begin to imagine how *much* bad luck.

It was Monday morning, and I had picked up my girl Jessa en route to school. I was still waking up, even after a big cup of coffee, because I'd stayed up late the night before helping Mikey Walters, one of the guys in the soccer team, with his history project. When he asked for help, I should have told Mikey, "You waited too long to start on the assignment, so deal with it." But I have trouble saying no to anyone. I guess it has to do with being popular—and wanting to stay that way.

Why does my reputation matter so much? If you've ever been on top of the school scene, you'll probably understand, because you'll know how addictive popularity is—stronger than a drug, as important as anything. I've never met anyone willing to give up top-dog status, not if they could help it. At the same time, it stinks always trying to be the best. Sometimes I wish I could just be me.

Jessa was sitting at my side in the front of my pickup as we bounced along a dirt road, and the whole cab was filled with that patchouli-and-honey smell she always has. Outside, fog lay on the ground in gray billows with the Ponderosa pines sticking up through it like pointy witch fingers. Even though I've gone down this road a hundred times, the gloom and mist made me shiver a little. And then the coyote glided out from the side of the road.

"Ooh!" Jessa's voice was a tiny squeak.

The creature ambled across the graded surface just a few yards in front of my truck, stepping into the headlights' circles of light as if he owned the

whole road. I've never seen an animal act so nonchalant. He gazed straight at me with glowing yellow eyes, then slunk west across the road toward Mount Humphreys.

West.

Wrong direction.

Jessa was saying how amazing it was, but I stopped her. "It's bad luck if Coyote crosses your path."

"Another of your old Native traditions?"

My mom is Jicarilla Apache, and my dad is Navajo. We grew up in Kinlání, what the Anglos call Flagstaff. Mom was real connected to traditional ways, Dad not so much, but I learned a lot from his family, who still live in Navajo Nation.

"Coyote is the trickster," I told Jessa. "If he crosses you, your life gets confused."

"That's a neat story." She gave me one of her cute little smiles, but it didn't seem so cute to me right now.

"Not just a story," I said. "There are reasons for all the traditional Diné beliefs. Something bad is gonna happen. You should take this seriously."

"Don't be so uptight, Ken." She leaned close and nibbled at my ear. "Forget about that silly animal."

Any sane, red-blooded guy would have put the truck in park and done just that. I asked myself, Ken Benally, what's wrong with you? Grab your girl and forget about Coyote. But I couldn't. Coyote doesn't show up just by coincidence, and it was totally unnatural how he stared at me. Critters don't act like that.

But I did put the truck in park. Then I reached across Jessa, opened the glove compartment, and took out a little leather bag. "Wait a minute," I said to Jessa as I got out of the truck.

"What are you doing?"

"Corn pollen, it'll restore balance," I called over my shoulder. Stooping to see Coyote's tracks illuminated by the headlights, I poured a little pollen in each print. I hoped things would be okay after that.

But they weren't. The Trickster had signaled the start of a game—and I was about to be the pawn.

A couple of hours later, I was in Mr. Chesterton's science class. Mr. C is a big, red-haired guy that everybody loves, one of those teachers who really cares about each of his students. I wish every instructor were like him.

He was pointing to the screen behind him, which was covered with a big picture of a Jicarilla dance basket. "When tourists think of Native art, they usually think of jewelry, pottery, and Kachina dolls," he explained, "but some of the most unique—and sophisticated—Southwest tribal art is basketry."

"Natural fibers don't break if you drop them," Jessa agreed. "Makes them good stuff for plates and bowls."

"But I wouldn't run 'em through the dishwasher," Maeve Murphy retorted. She's a smart mouth who always dresses in black, like a punker turned vampire, but I have to admit, she makes the school—and our Crime Scene Club—a lot more interesting.

Jessa stuck her tongue at Maeve, behind Mr. C's back.

I was only half-listening. After all, this was old hat for me, because my mom is a traditional artist. Mom and Dad divorced four years ago, but before that, our house was filled with all sorts of shoots, reeds, branches, and bark, along with Mom's woven creations. After they got in that last big fight, Mom pretty much disappeared from my life, along with all her natural fibers and basketry. The house looks a lot more masculine and orderly now, pretty much what you'd expect of the house of a brass-tacks police sergeant.

Mr. C was saying, "Tonight, at the Northern Mountain Museum you'll have a rare opportunity to see the biggest and best display ever of Apache basketry. It's not well known, but the Northern Mountain Museum has the world's largest collection of Apache woven vessels. In addition, several prestigious institutions—including the Heard Museum in Phoenix and several tribal collections—have agreed to lend NMM their pieces. The exhibit opens at 7 this evening with a speech by the curator. Because I think this is valuable, I'll give extra credit to any student I see at the exhibition tonight."

"Hey, Mr. C." Maeve put up her hand. "I wanna come tonight but my car sort of got demolished in the last Crime Scene case."

That was an understatement; I saw the twisted, burnt wreckage that was left after her car went over that cliff. As a result of the accident, Maeve still wore a cast, now entirely covered with her creepy sketches.

"I'll pick you up," Sean offered. He's the nephew of our club sponsor, Detective Kwan. "Assuming that Aunt Dorothy gets home in time for me to use her car." Sean's this punk kid from down in Phoenix who came up here to get out of trouble. I'm thinking he and Maeve have something going but I don't know that for sure. The two of them make a scary duo. I sometimes wonder if Maeve thought CSC was a club for committing crimes, rather than solving them, when she volunteered to join.

"Don't worry about those two," a tall, thin boy with long blond hair and round glasses spoke up from the back of the room. Wire's this geek genius who could probably hack into the Pentagon at the same time that he's playing Warcraft on his PDA. "I'll pick up both Maeve and Sean on my way into town."

"Excuse me," Lupe Arellano said. "Could someone give me a lift up to the museum, too?"

"I'll pick you up," I offered.

"*We'll* pick you up," Jessa corrected.

Lupe and Jessa: those two girls are the conundrum of my life. I've been going with Jessa for almost two years now; she's in most of my classes, and my rock band, and she wears my ring on a leather string around her neck. All the guys say how lucky I am to have a girl like that. And I am. It's not just about physical attraction either; lots of good-looking girls go to Flag Charter, but Jessa has something more. I guess you'd call it an inner beauty, a largeness of soul. It's hard to describe, but she's strong in ways that I'm not and she fills in the missing pieces of my life. But . . .for some reason, I can't stop thinking about Lupe.

For almost a year, I've tried to ignore these feelings, pretend they weren't there. But then I admitted to myself, *I have a thing for that girl.* Lupe doesn't score very high in terms of popularity, but there's something about her sincerity and her smarts. I feel calmer when I'm around her, and I keep wishing I could hug her and tell her how amazing she is. But that would hurt Jessa terribly, and she no way deserves such a betrayal. So, Jessa's my girl. But I think about Lupe. Way too much.

After school, I put my books in the locker and headed back to Mr. C's room for Crime Scene Club. Lately it's gotten a kind of difficult being in CSC and soccer; practice and club meetings overlap too much. When they conflict, the club usually wins—but the guys on the team are getting frustrated with the situation. I try to imagine: What if Pelé had decided to skip soccer for some club? The answers that come to mind in response to that question tell me that skipping soccer practice is not a good move for my sports career.

On the other hand, what if Sherlock Holmes had gone nuts over sports rather than crime fighting? The club is a pretty cool opportunity, a partnership between the local police department and our charter school. Five of us were chosen out of dozens of applicants to be in the club. We get to work with real CSIs and use their equipment to solve actual cases. So maybe I should just drop soccer—but that wouldn't make me very popular with my team-mates.

There I go again, trying to keep everyone happy.

So while I have these ongoing arguments with myself, I keep going to both soccer and Crime Scene Club. On this particular day, the usual people were already at CSC when I arrived: Maeve was flipping through the pages of a tattoo magazine; Wire was tapping away at his PDA; Jessa and Lupe sat behind the first table in the room, on opposite ends. I pulled up a stool and sat between them.

A few moments later, Ms. Kwan entered. She's a detective with the local PD and their liaison for Crime Scene Club. "First of all," she began, "Let's have a round of applause to welcome Maeve back from the hospital. I know she's been in school a few days, but this is the first time we've all been together here at CSC."

We all clapped. Maeve deserved it.

"Next case, I think we should pull straws to decide who gets to drive their car over a cliff," Maeve retorted. "But I'm writing a short story in creative writing class, about a hot guy who kills his girlfriends by sabotaging their cars."

"Taking a break from vampire fiction?" I asked.

"Oh, no. The girls come back to life and suck his blood."

"I just don't dig this whole Goth thing," Jessa sighed.

"That last case would make a great video game," Wire suggested. "I know some guys in Tokyo who

might be interested in the idea. It could be a car-chase-slash-shooter game; we could create an animé Maeve and. . ."
"Getting back on track," the detective continued, speaking loudly to reestablish her authority, "there are concerns about the safety of this club, both from the police department and from our school board. So I want you to carefully read, sign, and follow this expanded list of Safety Promises for CSC."

I skimmed over the handout. It was all common-sense stuff:

> *1. I will not involve myself in any form of criminal investigation without the explicit permission of CSC sponsors.*
> *2. I will not involve myself in any situation where I could be harmed or draw the attention of criminals for any reason, whatsoever.*

The list went on and on. I signed at the bottom. And I meant it. I intended to stay out of trouble.

So how come I violated almost every rule of the Safety Promises in the following week? Temporary insanity is probably the best plea, but I blame Trickster Coyote.

After everyone signed the new rules—while Maeve rolled her eyes and Wire smirked—Ms. Kwan plugged her laptop into the projection system. "I want to introduce you to one of our basic tools," she said, "The Ident-a-Criminal computer art system. For over a hundred years, investigators have attempted to create visual images of perpetrators, based on eyewitness descriptions. At first, crime investigators needed to have a sketch artist available, to draw a picture based on witness interviews. Later, we developed jigsaw-puzzle-style identification kits, with hundreds of different eyes, noses, mouths, hair styles, and so on that could be pieced together to create a composite image of the suspect."

"Kind of like your very own Jack-the-Ripper Mr. Potato Head." Maeve gave an evil chuckle.

I was pretty sure Detective Kwan bit back a smile, but all she said was, "Nowadays we have software that works similar to the old puzzle kits, only with tens of thousands more options for better results. Using computer simulation, we can create likely portrayals of a person as they age. So the computer can sketch how a person looks today, even if he or she went on a missing-person list as a child, decades ago. Or, we can reconstruct how a victim looked when alive, even if the only remains are a skull and bones."

At this point, while Jessa, Wire, and Maeve got into a big argument over the relative merits of a human artist versus the computer program, my mind drifted. I have to admit I was thinking instead about the relative merits of the two girls sitting beside me. On the one hand, there was Jessa—sexy, dreadlocked, artistic, nature-scented Jessa—and on the other hand, there was Lupe, with straight long hair like my own, with this amazing brilliant mind. My attention to the meeting totally faded away as I daydreamed about first one girl, then the other. The next thing I knew, Ms. Kwan was dismissing us.

Jessa wanted to hang out at the library until the museum event, so I dropped her off and then realized how hungry I was. Dad was working second shift, which meant I was on my own for supper.

Night was falling, and thunder rumbled in the distance as I headed down Old Route 66 to Scorsese's Pizza Parlor. They're open 24 hours and sell big hot slabs of pizza for just two bucks a slice, with free refills of soda. My kind of place. But when I walked into Scorsese's, I froze, staring at the three people standing in line: two men—a white guy with a big scar on his cheek and a goatee, and a Latino with a cowboy hat and mustache—and a woman who looked just like my mom.

She was in her mid-forties, stocky but fit, with long, slightly wavy hair, thin nose, strong chin, and deep, wise eyes. She wore jeans and a red hooded sweater, just like Mom used to wear. *But what would Mom be doing in Flagstaff?* Last I'd heard, she was living in Albuquerque, working for the Bureau of Indian Affairs there, and—according to my Dad, who was still seething about it—living with some guy. Mom and I hardly ever spoke, and I hadn't seen her in about four years. She called me on my birthday and Christmas, occasionally sent forwards from her office e-mail. My awareness of Mom was mostly the sense of her absence.

I took a breath, trembling. "Mom?"

Her eyes widened.

For an instant, I was sure it was her. Then the white guy said, "Who's the kid?"

The woman's eyes narrowed. "Some boy who thinks I'm his mother." She gave me a little smile. "You're confusing me with someone else." Then she turned to her two companions. "Let's get out of here."

They left. They didn't even wait for their pizza.

I put a hand on the wall to steady myself. She looked like Mom and she sounded like Mom. But why would Mom deny that she knew me?

People can change a lot in four years. Who knows what Mom looks like now? Maybe Mr. Chesterton talking about Apache weaving had triggered a desire to see Mom, so I just latched onto the face of this total stranger. Maybe crossing Coyote had spooked me even more than I'd realized.

I'd lost my appetite, so I turned around and went out to sit in my truck, staring at the streetlights and the full moon rising. Seeing this woman who looked like Mom made me realize how much I missed her. Life with just Dad and me in the house pretty much sucks. But I don't like to think about that.

An hour later, Jessa, Lupe, and I sat in a big room at the Northern Mountain Museum. The meeting room was designed to impart a dark, dramatic mood. Faux torches on the wall were perched atop someone's art-deco notion of Pueblo art: I'll bet money they were designed in the 1920s. The room was in blackness, apart from the narrow shafts of light that fell on big, square objects covered with black drapes, display cases full of art, waiting to be unveiled. Haunting flute music added to the atmosphere; the air was heavy with the breathless sense that something mysterious and exotic was about to be revealed.

The small auditorium was filled with lots of Native people and a smattering of older, wealthier whites. Funny, after five centuries destroying my heritage, the European-American elite have apparently decided Indian art is very cool. I shouldn't be mad, though, because wealthy *bilagáana* (that's white folk in Diné) pay good money to artists like my mother.

There I go again, thinking about Mom. My head's really screwed up.

Meanwhile, the curator was beginning his lecture. He had a baby face, short blond hair, and thick black-rimmed eyeglasses. He wore a grey suit with a bolo tie, and he talked with a squeaky voice. "Behind me," he motioned to the display cases covered with black cloths, "are several dozen outstanding examples of a vanishing art: Apache basketry."

"Dude, what's with this guy?" whispered Sean in my ear. He was leaning forward from the row behind us.

"I saw him on the public access station once, talking about dinosaurs, totally corny," Wire muttered on the other side of me.

"Shut up!" Lupe whispered.

The museum guy went on to explain how Native people in the Southwest had developed techniques for weaving baskets, plates, and other utensils for

practical reasons, making them beautiful as an expression of "everyday sacredness." He concluded, "We now recognize these functional vessels as extraordinary examples of decorative art. And thus the Northern Mountain Museum's collection alone is valued at half a million dollars."

I was having a hard time listening. Like I said, I've heard all about these things since I was a kid. But what really made it hard to concentrate was the fact that Lupe had accidentally brushed her hand over mine. Or was it accidental? I turned and looked at her. She had on a tight black top, and she was wearing lipstick . . . and then I realized Jessa was pressing so hard against my other side, I thought she'd cut the circulation off at my elbow. I turned toward her, and watched her lip curl down in a little pout that was totally sexy. What's a guy to do when he's stuck between two equally incredible girls?

The audience was clapping, and I looked back toward the speaker. He turned sidewise, pointing toward the covered cases with a theatrical gesture. "Ladies and gentlemen, I give you—masterpieces of traditional Apache art."

The dark cloth covers pulled upward on ropes, like stage curtains lifting toward the ceiling, revealing the glass cases beneath.

There was a sudden silence.

The cases were empty.

Chapter 2
FAMILIAR FACE

Tuesday morning, the first thing I felt was a big slobbery tongue on my face. My German shepherd Bandit lapped my cheek, his way of asking for his breakfast. I wiped off the saliva with the sleeve of my sweatshirt and headed toward the kitchen.

For a few moments, I was actually thinking that everything that had happened yesterday had been a dream. But as soon as I entered the dining room, I knew it had all been real. Dad was up and dressed in his uniform, sipping a big cup of coffee and reading this morning's issue of the *Northern Sun* newspaper. I could read the headline from across the room: PRICELESS NATIVE ARTIFACTS STOLEN!

But Dad turned to the sports section. "I see Flag Charter's soccer team is number two in the state."

"Yeah, we're pretty good, huh?"

Dad looked up and scowled. "Are you kidding? How come you're number two? What's wrong with you?"

I pulled a box of cereal out of the cupboard and tried to pretend his words didn't sting.

"There are two kinds of people, son—the best and the losers. You don't want to be a loser, do you?"

I've heard that line a million times, so I didn't even roll my eyes this time. "No, Dad."

"Better get your game together."

I nodded, but inside I was steaming. It wouldn't matter if I was the world champion of soccer, had a number-one hit on the radio, and discovered the cure for cancer; I still wouldn't measure up to my father's standards.

He flipped back to the front page of the paper. "You were at the museum last night, weren't you?"

I nodded.

"Any insight into the crime?"

I shook my head. "The curtains lifted, the display cases were empty, and then they cleared the place out."

Truth was, I really wasn't thinking that much about the crime. The woman at the pizza place was a bigger mystery for me than the theft. Could Mom be in town for some reason? If so, why would she act like she didn't know me? If it wasn't Mom, why did someone else look so much like her? Did I have an identical aunt no one ever told me about?

There's no way I can ask Dad all these questions; he hasn't said a kind word—or even a neutral word—about Mom since the divorce. It was like in Dad's mind, Mom became someone else after she left us, the personification of evil. I knew if I mentioned the woman that looked like his former wife, Dad would go off on a tirade, and I didn't want to start my day listening to that.

"How's Crime Scene Club?" Dad asked.

I told him about the computer imagery software, and the discussion the club had had whether hand-drawn forensic art might be better.

"That's a crap-shoot," he told me. "It depends on the artist. They're like profilers. Sometimes it almost seems like there's some kind of spiritual connection between a crime artist and the criminals they draw."

"That's spooky," I told him.

"Sure is."

That day, school dragged along, and my attention kept drifting. Finally, the last bell rang, and it was time for Crime Scene Club. Unfortunately, Coach Peterson decided the soccer team needed an extra practice at the same time.

As I shoved my books in my locker, Mikey from the soccer team said, "Hey, aren't you coming to practice?"

"Sorry, CSC meeting. Can't do both."

Mikey slapped his hand against the lockers. "Come on, Benally! Coach says you miss one more time and you're off the team. We're just a shot away from number one. Don't you care? How can you do this?"

I hate no-win situations. Worse, I hate letting people down, and this was going to let the team down big-time. But CSC is an amazing thing, something that probably doesn't exist anywhere else in the country, and it's going to look great on a college application. This was one tough decision, and for a few seconds I just stood there staring at Mikey, like a deer in the headlights of an oncoming six-wheeler.

I sighed. "Sorry, Mikey, I'm going to club." I didn't wait around to hear his response; I just turned and hurried down the hall toward Mr. Chesterton's room.

Ms. Kwan came in right behind me, all excited that the PD had agreed we could investigate the case of the stolen artifacts. She handed out finely detailed black-and-white drawings of the missing baskets. I recognized some of the designs: a feathered serpent, thunder-and-lightning symbols. One of the weavings was the "man in the maze" design, with a little male figure trapped in a labyrinth. It's supposed to represent our spiritual journey through life, but today it seemed like a picture of me: confused and frustrated at every level.

"Why are you passing out drawings?" Wire asked. "Wouldn't photos be better?"

"As much as technology enthusiasts like you resent it," the detective replied, "line drawings of objects with tiny variations—fibers and designs like these baskets—are easier to work from than photographs would be. Neither film nor digital images capture distinctive details like these drawings do. So we're distributing these to every trading post, art gallery, and pawnshop in the Southwest. The most likely motive for stealing these baskets is to sell them—and these 'artifacts wanted' posters, along with a significant financial reward, should make it much harder to fence the stolen goods."

"What about the crime scene?" Lupe wanted to know. "Did the thief leave any physical traces?"

"We found a couple of partial prints on the glass, but they're not good enough to pull up a match on the national fingerprint registry," Ms. Kwan replied. "We also have a few long, black fibers that look like human hair. If that proves to be the case, once we have a suspect in custody, they will be wonderful for a positive ID. But they're no good until we have a hair sample to match with the one we found."

"So," Maeve asked, "where do we start our investigation? Want me to go undercover and act like an art expert?"

Everyone in the room chuckled, remembering how Maeve had infiltrated the Extremez car club—and picked up a handsome male suspect—on our last case.

Ms. Kwan shook her head. "No, Maeve. First, I'm not sure how credible you'd be in the Native art scene—but more important, that would violate our new safety rules."

Maeve wrinkled her nose and looked disappointed.

"Back to your original question, however," the detective continued, "we begin by looking for our primary suspect, since we do have a visual lead."

"We do?" Lupe sounded excited.

Ms. Kwan nodded. "There was a woman, middle-aged, who showed up late in the afternoon and told the NMM caretaker she was from the Heard Museum. She said she needed to inspect the installation before the show. There was no reason for him to doubt her, especially when she made a few knowledgeable comments about Apache basketry. So he didn't think much more about her. Apparently, she was the last person in the room before the baskets came up missing. Of course, the staff at NMM called the Heard afterward. Turned out they hadn't sent up anyone."

"She's the thief, all right." Wire stated the obvious.

"Sounds like a good use for your Ident-a-Criminal program," Lupe said.

"You're right," Ms. Kwan agreed. "Look at this."

She handed out a colored image: a computer-generated portrayal of the suspect, based on the janitor's description.

As soon as I saw it, I felt queasy. "Ms. Kwan?"

"Yes, Ken?"

"Did the janitor say what our suspect was wearing?"

"She wore jeans and a dark red fleece sweater with hood."

For a moment, it was hard to breathe. Then my head cleared, and I realized that lots of people wear fleece sweaters.

"Any description of her vehicle?" Lupe asked.

"The caretaker saw her get into a Ford F150, white, with chrome wheels," the detective replied.

I don't have any idea what Mom is driving these days. Four years ago she had a Volvo, but it was on its last legs, so by now she'd have something else. My mind spun, trying to make sense out of everything, trying to sort it all out so that it added up to something different, anything other than that my mom was a thief.

"Hey, Ms. Kwan," Jessa offered, "Do you think the department could arrange for me to meet the museum's janitor and make a sketch of the suspect, from his description? It might not hurt to try a human artist—not just rely on the computer."

"That's a good idea, Jessa. I'll call right away and see if we can arrange for you to make a sketch tomorrow."

I looked down at the computer image of the suspected thief. It didn't exactly look like my mother, but it was darned close. If someone handed me that picture and asked, "Who does that look like?" I wouldn't hesitate to answer, "My mom."

I didn't tell anyone my fears about Mom and the crime. If it was some woman who just happened to look like Mom, everyone would think, "Ken's a nutcase who thought his own mother was a criminal." And if Mom—for some unfathomable reason—was involved with the crime, then it would be, "Ken, he's the creep who ratted out his own mother." Either way, I'd look like a loser.

Of course, Jessa picked up that I wasn't feeling right. She kept asking, "Ken, what's the matter?" But I couldn't tell her.

I went home and went to bed early, trying hard not to think about anything at all. Maybe everything would magically work out by itself tomorrow.

But the next day started just as bad. Bandit woke me with his smelly, slobbery greeting, and then as soon as I went downstairs, Dad lit into me.

"Coach Peterson called and said you missed too many practices. They're headed for state and you got yourself kicked off the team!"

"I'm sorry, Dad, I—"

"How on earth can you be so stupid?" he interrupted.

"But I had to pick between soccer and CSC, and they wouldn't—"

"Why can't you do both?" He seemed determined to not let me finish a sentence.

"I ... I just can't. It's not possible..." This time my voice trailed away on its own, while he just shook his head and scowled at me.

"Where there's a will, there's a way," he finally said when I didn't say anything more. "You didn't try hard enough."

I almost exploded then. I wanted to scream at him that I try as hard as I can all the time, but it'll never be good enough for him. I didn't say anything, though. I just poured myself a cup of coffee and took it back to my room.

That afternoon at Crime Scene Club, Ms. Kwan passed around the portrait of the suspect Jessa had sketched, based on Jessa's interview with the museum custodian.

"I tried to get a sense of her personality from the caretaker, not just her outward appearance," Jessa explained. "He said she appeared confident but

reserved, knowledgeable about the artwork but not arrogant. In his words, 'she didn't wear her smarts on her sleeve the way some people do.' I thought about those qualities while I made the sketch."

"What Jessa did is typical of the best forensic artists," Detective Kwan said. "They try to capture the inner essence of a perpetrator—and that's why some people think that hand-drawn portraits are still valuable in crime work, because no computer can generate that added human element. Incidentally, the museum worker confirmed that Jessa really did a good job capturing his perception of the woman's personality."

All this time, I still hadn't seen what the drawing looked like, but at this point, Lupe handed me a copy of the picture and the room seemed to tilt for a few seconds.

Now it *really* looked like Mom.

I heard Ms. Kwan say, "We may have another break in this case." She motioned toward her laptop's monitor, where we could see a blurry image that looked like three people in a store. "We had a little time between our sketching session and this meeting, so Jessa and I decided to make a quick circuit of local businesses with this sketch. The clerk at Mountain View Convenience Store said that our woman, along with two male companions, stopped there the same night those baskets were stolen. He gave us a surveillance tape. It's pretty grainy, but. . ." She tapped at the keys on her laptop. "We can do a lot to improve this. Are any of you familiar with video enhancement technology?"

I knew who was going to answer, before Wire said a word. "Wasn't that developed by NASA for weather satellites in the late nineties?" he asked.

"It was indeed," the detective affirmed. "Turns out technology made for outer space helps us solve crimes in a down-to-earth way." She tapped a few more keys. "How's this?"

The blurry images sharpened, and for the second time in just a few minutes, I felt dizzy. I recognized the Latino with the hat and mustache, and the white guy with a big scar and goatee. And there was the woman who looked like Mom.

"Any match with databases?" Lupe asked.

"Good question." Ms. Kwan nodded her approval at Lupe. "There are a number of online databases with criminal mug shots, and several programs that match up pictures of suspects with these databases. It's not exact, but it works pretty good. So we ran several programs. No match on the woman, but these two"—she pulled out a laser pointer that danced around the men's faces—"are Hector Rubio" (she indicated the man with the hat) "and Joe Sandy" (scar face).

Lupe shuddered. "I wouldn't want to meet Sandy in a dark alley."

"Rubio's kinda cute, though," Maeve whispered loud enough for everyone to hear.

"Gross me out," Jessa retorted.

Detective Kwan ignored them. "These guys have outstanding warrants in Texas, New Mexico, and Colorado, for drug possession and transporting stolen goods. They both reside in Albuquerque, and of course neither are at home. We've attained warrants for the city police to search their places, see if they left any clues to their current where-abouts."

"Is there anything more we can do here?" asked Wire.

"We'll distribute these pictures—with the names of our two 'wanted' criminals and the anonymous woman, whom we'll call 'person of interest' for this case. Hopefully we'll get some sightings soon."

I know I should have said something, right then and there. I still didn't know whether the woman I had seen was my mother—but I'd seen these three together. But I didn't say anything.

You might be wondering, "How could a police-man's son withhold evidence?" All I can say is, What would you do if you thought your mother might be involved in a felony? Could you rat on your mom?

The next day I managed not to obsess about the crime or my mother, because my band, Red, White, and Blues, had a performance in the evening. The school orchestra teacher lets us practice in his room before shows, so I was busy that morning loading up amps and cables in my truck, and then unloading them at school. During study hall and lunchtime we practiced. Jessa was almost giddy with excitement; she gets that way before shows.

Then, after school, it was load the truck again and drive to our gig at a place called South of the Tracks. It was a full day just getting ready for the show, and I was glad for that.

By eight PM, the club was filled. It was an all-ages show, so a lot of the Flag Charter kids were in the room. Backstage, we huddled briefly. All of us—Sticks, the flat-topped, muscle-bound kid who plays drums; Carlos, the constantly smiling lead guitar player; Jessa who does vocals; and me, the guy on the rhythm guitar and bass—were amped up, figuratively as much as literally. We ran out on stage and the audience screamed.

There's something about performing to a big room full of ecstatic music fans that brings out a whole different me. Most of my life, I have to think about my actions. I'm constantly asking myself if I'm doing the right thing or not. Will this make people happy? Will that make them mad at me? It gets exhausting, always working to stay on top. But it's different performing with the band; it just happens like magic. No thinking, just being. It's not calculated, it's real.

Sticks started tapping out a beat, and I plucked at the strings on the bass. We had incredible reverb on the soundboard as the band launched into our re-make of that old Led Zep tune, "Dazed and Confused." Jessa swayed back and forth while we laid down the beginning chords, then she pulled the mic off its stands and up to her lips. Something happens to that girl when she gets on stage to sing. You can take all those twenty-something female celebrity singers with their overnight marriages and car crashes and alcohol rehabs; they don't hold a candle to Jessa's talent. Her voice is so rich, powerful, so full of soul. The crowd was swaying, waving their hands, screaming, all through that first song. And that was just the opening number.

An hour later, we had reached our encore, with Jessa belting out "Piece of My Heart." The veins popped out of her neck and her whole body shook, like she was squeezing out every drop of anger and angst in her soul, right through the speakers. The rest of us were working our instruments like there was no tomorrow, and the whole club was in a daze.

Toward the end of that amazing, glittering moment, my gaze narrowed in on Lupe in the center of the room, leaning back on a railing, staring at me. She had curled her hair, put on sparkling make-up, and taken her glasses off. I couldn't take my eyes off her. For this crazy moment, it was like everything went silent, and it was just she and me, looking at each other. That may be the instant when something inside me finally just shattered, like a piece of glass being hit by a rock.

Like I've already told you, I've spent my whole life trying to do, say, and act right, so I really can't explain what happened. Was it Coyote's curse? Or was I just stupid?

Sticks brought the song to a crashing crescendo, matching Jessa's spine-tingling wails. The audience screamed and clapped. We all stepped forward, held hands, bowed together, and waved. Then we went backstage. What a rush. Man, we were good. But even though the clapping was still going, no one felt like going back for another encore.

"I gotta get some air and let my head clear out." Jessa said. "Catchya in ten minutes, okay?" She vanished out the exit without waiting for a reply.

I leaned back against the side of the hallway, taking deep breaths, soaking in the good feelings, trying to forget that weird moment with Lupe. And then—she was right there, in front of me. "You were incredible!"

I *tried* to do the right thing, honestly, at least at first. "We're incredible because of Jessa," I said. "She's the real talent in this band."

Lupe mouth drooped. "I didn't come here to talk about Jessa."

I glanced left, then and right. No one else was in the hallway. My heart was suddenly pounding. I knew something was about to happen, and once it did, there would be no undoing it.

"I've been wanting to tell you," Lupe said, "since that moment in the canyon when were alone, and—"

I couldn't wait for her to finish. I'd been waiting too long.

I grabbed her and kissed.

She pulled back for a moment, looked at me with huge startled eyes, then she took a step forward and put her mouth against mine. . . .

"Hey!"

Jessa. For a few moments, the three of us stood, frozen, silent.

There was something in Jessa's expression I had never seen before, a look way deeper and worse

than anger. Then she pulled hard at the cord around her neck, snapped the leather string, and held out my ring in her hand.

I didn't move.

"Take it," she snapped.

When I still didn't move, she picked up my hand and slapped the symbol of our commitment into my palm. "We're finished." Without another word, she strode down the hallway.

I turned back toward Lupe.

"That was so wrong," she blurted.

I reached out to touch her, but she stepped away from me, shaking her head, then turned and ran away. When she glanced back at me just before she went out the door, I saw silver tracks on her cheeks

I was alone.

Chapter 3
PERSON OF INTEREST

I didn't want to face the next day, but you can only stay in bed so long. If I had known what awaited me at the breakfast table, though, I might never have come out of my room.

Rubbing my eyes, I stumbled into the kitchen and breathed the scent of fresh-brewed coffee. Dad was seated at the table, a big pile of scrambled eggs in front of him. He motioned toward the coffee-maker. "Want some?"

I helped myself, feeling a moment of hope. Maybe this day would somehow go better than all the others recently.

But then my dad said, "Sit down. We need to talk."

My stomach knotted, and my appetite disappeared. Bandit whined under the table, as though he sensed the tension in the room. Sometimes I think animals seem more human than people do. I took a chair and pressed my legs against his furry warmth for comfort.

Dad sucked in a breath. "Your mom is a suspect in this case."

I tried to feign shock.

Dad gave me a disgusted look. "Don't pretend you're surprised. You saw the pictures and you knew the facts. You're not stupid."

I was afraid to ask, but I had to know. "Dad, did you tell the department that the woman on the posters is Mom?"

Dad rubbed his hand across his face. "Think it was easy? But I pledged myself to serve and protect. That's what I do."

"But you don't know it was Mom. Lots of women look a bit like her."

He didn't say anything, just sat there eating his breakfast, his face as hard as a stone.

"Dad, all we have is the artist's sketch, and you know how unreliable those are." I didn't bother to mention that the artist happened to be my now-former girlfriend. "Forensic art narrows the list of possible suspects from thousands to dozens, but it's just the artist's idea of what a person might look like. It's not an exact science—only guess-work. And even if the police provide a photograph, lots of people come forward with false leads. In big cases, they'll get a hundred callers saying, 'That's him—I saw the wanted poster,' and they'll rat on their neighbor or coworker or estranged sibling. But ninety-nine percent of them are *wrong*."

Dad took another sip of his coffee. His face didn't change at all.

I scrambled for the right words to convince him. "I know you hate her, for what she did to you— what she did to us—but that's no reason to jump to conclusions. It could be a total fluke that the picture resembles her. And it could be the woman at the museum was someone else who just happens to look like Mom. Remember one year we went up to the Grand Canyon, and there was this little boy who looked just like me—looked so much like me that you and Mom both thought he was me until I came running up and you both just freaked and went on about how the other kid could be my twin? It happens, Dad. People look alike—and innocent folks get framed all the time because they resemble someone else."

He took another bite of egg, chewed, swallowed. "Done?"

"No! You might hate her guts—but she's still my mom. I love her, Dad, and when you try to hurt her . . . you hurt me too."

"I'm not trying to hurt her." His voice was flat, as hard as his expression.

"Oh, yeah?"

"I would never want to hurt your mother."

"Then why did you give her name to the cops, just because of a stupid piece of forensic art?"

"That wasn't all."

I stared at him, suddenly afraid to find out any more. "You did some investigating?" I asked slowly.

He nodded. "I called that creep she lives with in Albuquerque."

I winced, imagining what that conversation must have been like.

"I gave him a false name. If he'd known it was me, the jerk would've clammed up. He said she's out-of-town on a trip, something to do with her expertise in basketry. She left the day before the robbery."

I pressed my legs harder against Bandit.

"He can't reach her on the phone."

I stared down at my plate. I didn't know how my dad could eat. The eggs looked utterly disgusting, like chunks of something yellow and nasty.

"She was driving a white Ford F150." My father's voice was relentless. "With custom wheels."

"Those are…" My voice cracked and I tried again. "Those are pretty bad coincidences. But that's still not proof."

"You want to hear it all?"

I didn't move for a moment. Then I nodded.

"She had prints done for her job. She visits people in their homes, and BIA workers who do that need to have fingerprint background checks. You remember there were partial fingerprints taken from the empty glass cases at the museum?"

I didn't want to hear what he would say next.

"Partial prints can make a positive ID, when matched with full ones. Mom's prints were on that case. It's a sure match."

I tried to focus. "So . . . is there a warrant for Mom's arrest?"

"No. She's still just a 'person of interest, wanted for questioning.' But now that 'person of interest' has a name."

I picked up my coffee cup, put it down. I was pretty sure I'd gag if I tried to swallow anything.

"Ken."

I made myself meet my father's eyes.

"If you see your mother, you need to let me or someone else in authority know. Are we clear about that?"

I nodded. I understood.

But I had no intention of telling him.

After breakfast I paused for a minute to offer corn pollen and prayers, and then I drove to school. Alone.

I stared straight ahead at the road as I passed by Jessa's house. This was the first time in I don't know how long that I didn't pick her up.

I tried to avoid talking to anyone as I went into homeroom. I took a seat and stared at the television. Miss Rojas usually watches the local morning news in her room before the bell rings, and now the woman who anchors for KFLG was saying, "Police have identified three people wanted for questioning in the theft of valuable artifacts from the Northern Mountain Museum. Two are known criminals, Hector Rubio"—they flashed a mug shot—"and Joe Sandy"—another mug shot. "Rubio and Sandy are dangerous and should be approached with caution. A person of interest is also wanted for questioning in connection with the case, Ms. Stella Benally." They showed Jessa's sketch of my mom; I guess the station didn't have a photo yet. My dad must have given the police one, though. "If you see any of these people, call—"

Miss Rojas turned the television off.

Sam Gupta turned around in his seat and looked at me. "Hey, that woman they're looking for has your last name."

Why didn't she change back to her maiden name when she and Dad divorced?

"Yeah," Sally Rae said, "she looks a lot like you, too."

"Is she your aunt or something?" Sam asked.

But the bell rang then, and we all jumped up and made our way to whatever class we had first period.

Saved by the bell.

But not for long. We live in the information age, and by lunch hour someone read a news story on the computer that said that Ms. Stella Benally was divorced from Officer Victor Benally of the Flagstaff PD. It didn't take people long to figure out that meant she is also the mother of . . . me.

And since gossip travels faster than light speed at Flag Charter, before I could buy my lunch sandwich and soda, half the kids in school were pursuing me with questions like a pack of paparazzi on the trail of a celebrity.

"Ken, that's your mother on the news, right?"

"Is this why you quit the soccer team?"

"Think your mother's a big-time art thief?"

"How's it feel to be a cop's kid and have a criminal for a mother?"

I ran for the counselor's office. She offered to talk but I wasn't in the mood for that. So she let me spend some time alone in her room. That gave me a chance to reflect.

That didn't make me feel any better.

What *was* Mom doing with thugs like Rubio and Sandy? Mom is so moral she used to drive me crazy.

Once I tried smoking (just cigarettes, not pot even); she found out and I was grounded for two weeks. Does that sound like the kind of woman who would steal half a million dollars of art from a museum?

Maybe the man she lives with persuaded her to steal the baskets for money? But why would he have answered my dad's questions the way he did if he was behind the thing? I couldn't sort it out.

And unfortunately, Mom wasn't the only thing on my mind. Jessa was acting like I didn't exist. All morning, she pretended I wasn't there. I wished she would yell at me, or gossip, or do anything but this.

I hoped at lunch hour, when the whole school turned on me like a pack of rabid dogs, she would at least look at me, say one kind word, like, "I'm still mad about last night—but I want you to know that I'm sorry about your Mom." Yeah, right. She didn't even glance my way. When she'd said, "We're finished," she meant it, in every sense of the word. We're not even friends anymore.

And then there's Lupe. Sometimes my band sings that old hippy song, "If you can't be with the one you love, love the one you're with." I figured after Jessa dropped me, Lupe would pick me up. I mean, she's been waiting for that, right?

Nope. Not a word from Lupe, either. She wasn't as good as Jessa at giving me the cold shoulder, so I'd catch Lupe glancing in my direction, her forehead wrinkled, but she didn't say anything to me either.

I got a moment to talk to Maeve, before I hid in the office. I asked her, "You hear about last night?"

"Yeah, Sticks told the world."

"Great."

"You really screwed up."

"I know."

"Don't expect any sympathy from your singer girl—or the skinny one."

"I knew Jessa would be mad . . . but what's with Lupe?"

Maeve looked at me like I was an idiot. "You're a smart guy, Ken, but you don't know squat about girls."

Thanks, Maeve, you're a real help.

Dad always says, "Be a man. Face your fears." I've tried to do that my whole life. So after lunch, I unlocked the door and ventured to science class. I figured I'd be safe enough there in Mr. Chesterton's room.

Halfway through the class, Carlos, who sits behind me, whispered, "Dude! What we gonna do 'bout the show tonight?"

Hard to believe, but I'd forgotten: our gig at South of the Tracks was a two-nighter.

"Don't worry," I whispered over my shoulder. "Life stinks but I can still play guitar."

"I know that, but what about Jessa?"

"What do you mean?"

"She told Sticks she's quit the band."

"She's not singing tonight?"

"Not now, not ever. Says she's finished with Red, White and Blues."

Sometimes, when you feel like a truck ran over you, it backs up and crushes you again, with all eighteen wheels.

"What're we gonna do?" Carlos sounded panicked.

I thought for a moment, made sure Mr. C wasn't looking our way, then whispered back, "Don't worry, man. A lot of great groups reinvent themselves when they lose a member. I can sing pretty good, you can harmonize with me. We'll do Jessa's vocals. It'll be a new creative expression for the band."

"Sure that's gonna work?"

"Smooth as silk."

I so hate lying.

That night, just the three of us backstage seemed awful weird. It was even worse knowing that a hundred people were waiting in the club to see the son of an alleged criminal try to perform despite his embarrassment.

The club manager announced us and we ran out on stage, greeted by restrained applause. Before I even had my bass plugged in, someone shouted, "Where's Jessa?"

We launched into our first number, a defiant rendering of "We Used to Be Friends." It was a bad choice, because Carlos and I can't sing high enough for that song. When we finished, one or two people clapped. That's all. The silence coming up from the audience felt like something you could touch

By the time we did our third number, the fans—if you can call them that—weren't silent any longer. Instead, they started chanting in unison, "We want Jessa—we want Jessa."

After the fifth song, the crowd was booing and yelling insults. I couldn't take it. I set my guitar down, shrugged, and walked off stage.

Carlos and Sticks were both livid.

"Why did you mess it all up?" Carlos wanted to know.

Sticks stated the obvious: "We suck without Jessa."

"You had to mess around and ruin our band." Carlos was practically shouting at me. "We could've been great, we could have made it big time. What on earth is wrong with you?"

My life was going downhill fast. I had definitely fallen off the tight rope of popularity; in fact, seemed to me I was in free-fall. I hadn't even landed yet, and already it hurt as bad as I always feared it would.

As I climbed into the cab of my truck, flashes of lightning flickered across the dark sky. I slammed my door against the cold wind blew. And for a moment, I just sat there, not really sure what to do or where to go next. I was scared of facing the club-goers who were emptying into the streets, though, so I turned the key, tapped the gas, and set off toward home. Dad was working late shift again, which meant there'd be no real food waiting for me, so I stopped into a convenience store for a bag of chips and a soft drink. Comfort food.

The guy at the counter nodded to me, acknowledging my presence without being overly friendly. Maybe he recognized. Maybe he was thinking, "There's that kid whose mother is a crook." I headed down the row of packaged snacks.

The bell on the door rang as someone else came in the store. I glanced at him and froze.

Tall man, scarred cheek, goatee.

Joe Sandy.

I glanced toward the parking lot to see what he was driving: a white pickup with chrome wheels.

What should I do? That wasn't hard to answer in theory. I knew the drill well enough: I should wait till he left the store, then write down the license number of the truck, see what direction he was headed, get right on my cell, and tell Dad. I reached for my phone.

But then I had this all-too clear mental image of my mom behind bars, miserable, asking, "Son, how could you have put me here?"

So should I do nothing? That didn't seem right either. Why was Mom hanging out with a guy like this? I had to know. My curiosity pulled me stronger than my common sense or my instinct for self-preservation.

I peered past rows of potato chips and candy bars as the scar-faced man selected a can of chewing tobacco and paid for it at the counter, then exited toward the truck.

I ran out behind him. "Hey, Joe Sandy."

He whirled around. "Who're you?"

"Ken Benally. I want to know about my mom." I gulped. "I want to know what my mother's doing with you and Hector Rubio."

He glared at me a couple of moments, then turned and opened the truck door. He pulled out a baseball bat.

I hadn't lost all my common sense. I ran back into the store.

He followed with long quick strides.

"Hey, what's going on?" the store clerk cried.

I sprinted toward the restroom, with the tall man racing after me.

K-e-e-rash!

The aluminum bat arced just inches from the back of my head, demolishing the glass door of a case full of drinks. I ducked and dodged, but the narrow aisle didn't give me much move to evade his next swing. The bat sliced through the air and smashed into a six-pack of beer, just missing my neck. I grabbed the restroom door handle and threw myself inside, then shoved hard to shut the door.

It wouldn't go shut. Long, strong fingers held it open it from the other side.

Moments like that you don't think; you just do what you have to. I leaned close and bit his hand.

A burst of profanities exploded from the other side of the door. I slammed it shut, threw the bolt across.

He smashed at the door with the bat and swore even louder. The door shook, but the hinges held.

I shut my eyes and took heaving gasps of air.

Silence. I waited. Then a high-pitched voice came from the other side of the door: "You can come out now. He's gone, I called the police."

A trick? I waited a few more moments, then opened the door a crack, holding the handle with both hands in case I had to push it shut again.

The clerk was alone in the store. Scattered across the floor was broken glass and battered food items. I took two shaky steps and let the restroom door fall shut behind me.

Now what? Wait for the police and explain to Dad why I decided to confront a wanted criminal, rather than call him the way I should have? I could just imagine what he'd say. I was so tired of listening to his criticisms.

I ran out the door and jumped back in my truck.

Chapter 4
A STRANGE REFUGE

I sped away down the road. Where to now?

I didn't want to talk to Dad—and I needed a place to get away from everyone at school. There wasn't anyone who was on my side now, not my buddies from the soccer team, not my friends from the music scene, not anyone.

Then I had an idea. I drove north out of town and turned off the road just outside the city limits onto a side route. I'd only been this way once before, and I hoped memory would serve me.

The headlights illumined tall trees as I climbed over a ridge and then followed a rough dirt road that lead east. Five minutes later, I saw what I was looking for: a beige trailer, so old and faded it blended in with the bare dirt around it. I parked the truck and headed toward the trailer door.

A motion sensor light came on and a tiny, ultra-modern surveillance camera swiveled to follow me. Not exactly what you expect to see on a dwelling like this, but it didn't surprise me, knowing the occupant. I touched the button on an intercom beside the door.

A voice greeted me: "Well, it's the band-leader on the run. The authorities are looking for you—it's all over the police radio. What brings you to my humble abode?"

"I need a place to hide out for a while, get my head together."

"Getting your head together may be a lost cause," the voice on the intercom said. Then the door swung open.

Wire stood there and looked at me, a Coke in one hand, wearing an expression I was too tired to try to read. "If everyone's looking for you, and I let you hole up here, am I harboring a fugitive?"

"They're not saying I'm a criminal, are they?"

"No. According to the police radio I've been monitoring, they just want to talk to you about someone who is a criminal, who apparently chased you around a convenience store and smashed up the place."

"So I'm hardly a fugitive."

"Guess not," Wire agreed. "I was kind of hoping you were, though—it would make the whole thing more fun. I haven't got any space in here." He gestured behind him. "So you'll have to crash on the floor."

"No problem. I have a sleeping bag in the truck."

"All my stuff is top secret, so if you tell anyone what you see in here I'll have to kill you."

"They can stick needles under my fingers and I won't tell."

"What if Jessa said she'd take you back? Would you tell for her?"

"I'm only made of flesh and blood."

Wire grinned, stepped back from the door, and waved me inside. "Welcome to my world."

I'd picked Wire up for school once, so that's how I knew where his place was, but I'd never been inside his trailer before. He's an emancipated minor. I don't know whether his parents were abusive, or addicts, or just unequipped to parent a total genius. All I know is, he values his privacy, so I figured this would be the perfect place to hang out and be away from everyone. I stepped inside the trailer.

"Whoa!" I've seen a lot of wild home-decorating schemes, but nothing like this. The trailer seemed even smaller inside than it did from the outside. It was maybe fifteen feet long and seven feet across, but what made it seem even more claustrophobic was that every inch of space was covered with electronics. Old television sets and computer monitors showed a dozen different pictures at once: streaming videos from the Internet, role-playing games, news channels, and feed from the outdoor surveillance camera, combined into a mosaic of moving images. Speakers large and small were interspersed in the high-tech mess, playing sound from all these different channels, plus the police radio, several foreign short-wave bands, and techno-trance music. Lights flickered on computer towers, amplifiers, equalizers and other devices that I couldn't even identify. I stared at this maze of gadgetry, mesmerized.

"Like the décor?"

"I think I saw your place on the *X-Files* once."

"That was fake. Pretty lame. My equipment's real."

"Can you actually keep track of all this stuff at once?"

"Multi-tasking." Wire gave a modest grin. "It's the next step in evolutionary development."

"How can you afford all this equipment—if you don't mind my asking?"

"I'm on a couple of professional gaming teams. Let's just say: we usually win. I could make a fortune, if I didn't take time out for school and Crime Scene Club."

"With all this, you plan to go into law enforcement after you graduate?"

Wire shook his head. "CSC is just something to help me stay well-rounded. Beside, cracking crime cases is the ultimate game."

"Game?"

"Yeah. It's us versus the bad guys, like an RPG—only the stakes are higher." He shrugged. "Hey, make yourself at home. I've gotta log onto a StarBattles competition. They're just starting a new round in Seoul, Korea." He plopped down into a padded swivel chair, pulled a visor with built-in screens over his eyes, and started chattering into his Bluetooth.

I knew Dad would be still at work, so I figured this would be a good time to leave a message for him. I dialed home on my cell. "Hey Dad, it's Ken. I'm all right. Not hurt at all. I just don't feel like talking to anyone right now. Life's out of balance for me—I hope you understand—I need a day or two to think through things and I'll come back home. Don't worry about me. Later." Of course, he would still throw a fit, but at least he wouldn't be worried while he wanted to kill me.

After that, I realized how exhausted I was from everything that had happened on this crazy day. I got my sleeping bag from the truck, spread it out on the narrow floor space, and fell asleep to the sound of a dozen broadcast channels, while Wire urged on his teammates in cyber land.

Not much happened the next day until the evening. We ordered a pizza, and I tried playing a couple of video games, until I realized Wire would whip my butt in the first few minutes. Then he got into another big online competition and I just hung around watching all the monitors.

Around sundown I took a walk in the woods, and sat on a rock by a creek, collecting my thoughts. There wasn't much point in avoiding Dad any longer. I figured I would go back home in the morning, apologize for messing up the case, and tell him everything that had happened. Of course, he'd rake me over the coals, but I could deal with that.

As for Lupe and Jessa, that was harder to sort out. I wanted to beg Jessa to take me back, to rewind the tape to that moment after the concert. Then I'd remember what it had felt like to kiss Lupe. Maybe I should pursue her, tell her things were over with Jessa. Why shouldn't we date? But that would hurt Jessa.

I sighed. First, I'd sort out things with Dad and this case involving Mom. There would be plenty of time then to worry about the girls. That was my plan, such as it was.

But it didn't happen that way.

When I walked back in the trailer, Wire grabbed me and pulled me toward a speaker. The police dispatcher was relaying a sighting, I realized: the woman and two men whose images were all over the media, in a white truck like the one described on the news channels, had been seen a half hour ago turning off the highway to the canyon, onto forest road 225.

I stared at Wire. "That's just a few miles from here."

He nodded. "We're probably a good twenty minutes closer to that turnoff than the closest squad car is."

I pulled on my jacket and was ready to run out the door, but Wire stopped me, "Hey, think before you do anything. Don't you want to know where they're headed?"

"It just said. Road 225."

"You know how many *other* roads branch off that and loop around back and forth?"

I shrugged, frustrated, wanting to get moving.

Wire sat down and punched on a keyboard as though he had all the time in the world. A complex set of lines appeared on a monitor in front of him. "They could go a dozen directions—which means you and the police could spend all night looking," he explained. "But let's assume they're heading to some kind of hideout—because why would they just be driving around in the woods?"

He punched a few more keys, and a satellite view of the area appeared. "There's only one dwelling in the most recent satellite photo. Here to the left off the cinder cone." He pointed to a tiny square on the screen.

"Think that's where they are?"

He nodded. "I'd bet on it."

"Do the officers know that?"

"Not sure if they'll figure that out or not. They may not be taking the time to look at the satellite images. But I'll get on the phone and call Ms. Kwan."

"Now?"

Wire's eyebrows went up. "No." His voice dripped with sarcasm. "I thought I'd wait until next week."

I ignored him and headed for the door again.

"Hold on! Aren't you forgetting some things—like safety and sanity and all those promises we signed in club?"

"I'm just going to check the place out," I told him. "I won't do anything until the police arrive."

"Promise?"

"Scout's honor."

"Were you ever a scout?"

"Actually, I was."

"Okay," Wire agreed. "But don't do anything stupid. If any of us in CSC gets in trouble—like we have in the past two cases—the club is toast. You don't want to ruin it for everyone by playing hero."

"I know. I'll be careful."

"I'll call the rest of CSC after I call Detective Kwan. We'll follow the police up there."

"Okay." I was out the door at last, but then I turned back. "Hey Wire?"

"Yeah?"

"Thanks."

I headed out into the dusk. The air was cold, spitting rain, and I ran to the truck. What would I find at that hidden cabin up the road? Was I racing to the solution of this case, or rushing toward disaster? I only knew that my destiny, and Mom's, were about to intersect just up the road.

Chapter 5
I TRY TO BE THE HERO

As the sky grew steadily darker, I drove a short way up the highway, then turned off onto the dirt fire road. The raindrops were bigger now, coming faster, making it harder to see. Soon the huge pyramid-like shape of the volcanic cinder hill rose up to the right of the road; I turned off my lights and headed to the left, driving slowly through the dark. I didn't want anyone to see or hear me coming.

Through the rain, I saw faint light ahead. I parked the truck in a grove of pines and shut off the motor. It was really pouring now, and in the distance, thunder boomed and faraway lightning briefly lit the sky. I pulled the hood of my jacket up over my head and crept forward toward the cabin.

It was a small building: four walls and a tin roof, with a door facing the road and a window on the side I could see. There was an outhouse a few feet away from it, which meant the place probably didn't have any plumbing. I tried to think if any of this information was helpful, and meanwhile, I moved from tree to tree, taking care not to slip on the wet grass and mud. When I reached the last tree, about twenty feet from the cabin, I hesitated—then I sprinted across the open space to the window side of the tiny building. My heart hammering, I peeked inside.

Two men were seating at a rickety table playing on a video game set. The guy with the goatee, Joe Sandy, wore a pistol in a shoulder holster. The other man had his back turned toward me, but I was pretty sure it was Rubio. My eyes moved to the other side of the room, where my mom was seated.

I gasped and ducked down, afraid they would look up and see me. My mother was bound and gagged.

I leaned against the outside of the cabin, breathing as hard as if I'd been playing soccer for an entire game. What was happening? Were these guys forcing Mom to help them? But she'd seemed compliant enough the first time I saw them at Scorsese's. Was this a double-cross?

Whatever was going on, I had to act fast. Mom was in trouble. I knew the police were coming—but would their arrival help my mother or put her in worse danger? I opened my cell phone: no service. I had no way to alert the officers that they were coming into a hostage situation. It was up to me to do something. But how?

I crawled around the cabin to the door, hoping the rain and thunder would drown out any sounds I made. The storm was moving closer, so I waited until a peal of thunder and then carefully tried the doorknob.

It was locked.

I dropped back against the wall, trying to think. Then the door swung open, spilling a triangle of light into the wet darkness. I held my breath, hoping against hope that whoever was standing there wouldn't see me.

An instant later, Hector Rubio sprinted toward an outhouse. He didn't look behind his back. Obviously, he just wanted to get there in a hurry.

I glanced back at the door: it had swung shut again, but it probably wasn't locked now. Did I dare go inside? Sandy was armed, and no doubt he'd use that pistol if he saw me coming. But I might not get a second chance to rescue Mom.

I got down on my knees on the wet ground and crept back to the door, slowly turned the knob, and eased it open a crack. Holding my breath, I peeked inside. Sandy was still playing his video game, his face turned away from the door. Slowly, slowly, I crept inside the door. Mom's eyes widened. I put my finger to my lips, and she looked away, trying not to betray me with her glance. Her face was as white as I'd ever seen it.

I crawled silently across the floor, behind Sandy. This was it. Now or never. I sucked in a breath, and then in a single motion, I sprang up and pulled gun out of the holster. I could barely believe I'd done it, and my hand was shaking as he whirled around. Somehow, I managed to level the gun at his forehead.

I'd never held a gun pointed at anyone before, and I was more scared of having to pull the trigger than anything else at that moment. But I tried to keep my face from showing what I was feeling. "Not a sound," I said. "And no sudden moves. Untie my mom."

The guy gave me a look that made my stomach knot, but he walked over to Mom and undid her gag.

I took a step closer to her. "Mom, are you okay?"

She turned toward me, her eyes full of a message I couldn't read.

A second later, I felt a flash of pain, like lightning striking the inside of my head. Then everything went black.

Chapter 6
OUT OF THE FRYING PAN AND INTO THE FIRE

You're probably wondering how I could have been so stupid that I forgot about the other guy. I wonder about that, too. All I can say is, I was worried about Mom and scared stiff of the gun in my hand. It's not like I do this kind of thing every day, you know.

When I came to, I was lying on the floor next to Mom, my hands tied behind my back and a rag in my mouth. My head felt like it might explode, but I managed to turn it so I could see what was happening.

Everything looked pretty much the same, except Rubio was standing in the doorway now. He looked over his shoulder at Sandy. "She's here."

Sandy grunted. "I don't like being around that woman. She makes me nervous. How do we know she's not a double-crosser, like that one?" He gestured toward my mother. "How much do we really know about her?"

"We know she's gonna pay us a quarter mill. That's all I care."

Sandy shook his head. "I don't like working for a broad. She orders us around like she owns us. Just 'cause she hired us doesn't mean—"

But at that instant, Rubio stepped back and a woman entered the cabin.

I couldn't see her face that well, so I couldn't make out her age; when she spoke, she had a smok-

er's voice. She was wearing a red dress and high-heel shoes, and her hair was shoulder-length and blond. I was pretty sure I'd never seen her before.

She held a metal suitcase, which she promptly set on the card table and snapped open. Both men sucked in a greedy breath, like she'd just spread some delicious meal before their eyes.

"Satisfied?" the woman asked.

Hector Rubio grunted his agreement and snapped the case shut.

"I'm sure you won't mind if I take a minute to examine the merchandise?" the woman asked. She stepped across the floor to a stack of cardboard boxes that lined the wall opposite from Mom and me. The woman took the top box, set it on the table, and pulled out one of the missing Apache baskets. As she turned back toward the table, I finally got a good look at her face. I tried to make mental notes, listing all the details I would tell Jessa so she could draw this woman.

"We haven't touched the artifacts," Joe Sandy said. "We left 'em just like she packed 'em." He nodded toward Mom.

At the moment, we all heard the far-away sound of sirens. The three criminals exchanged looks. It was about time for the police to arrive.

"Are they headed this way?" Rubio asked.

"Of course they are, you idiot. They're probably looking for the boy." The woman shot a glare in my direction.

She began quickly stacking the boxes full of artifacts, while Joe Sandy snatched the case off the table. "What should we do with those two?" He pointed at Mom and me, then pulled his gun, which he had evidently recovered from my hand while I was unconscious.

The woman shook her head. "Nah, don't shoot them. Leave the boy but take the woman. I'll be out of the country in twenty-four hours. After that, kill her. But I want her to disappear like Hoffa did, that clear? That's a body I don't want ever found."

They both nodded.

"Now help me carry these baskets to my van. Move it!"

The three headed out the door. I looked at Mom, and she looked back at me. Seemed to me we had a whole conversation in those few silent seconds, a conversation that pretty much covered the past four years when we hadn't been together. I could see the love in her eyes, and I hoped she could see its reflection in mine.

Then the two criminals grabbed her and dragged her out the door. Alone in the cabin, my eyes burning with tears, I listened as the sirens' whine drew closer.

A few minutes later, the door flew open, and Dad leapt inside with three other policemen. As soon as they took the gag out of my mouth, I shouted, "There are two men and a woman. They just left in two separate vehicles. You have to catch them— they have Mom and they're going to kill her!"

Dad insisted on staying with me, but the other officers took off after the thieves. The rain pounded on the tin roof in a strange rhythm that made me think of Sticks playing drums in a bad mood.

Dad dropped into one of the rickety chairs, staring at me. I could tell he wanted to chew me out, but this wasn't the time or place.

"Can't we follow them?" I asked, desperate to do something to help my mom.

He shook his head. "There's a bump the size of an egg on the back of your head. I've called for an ambulance and you're not going anywhere till it arrives." I knew I'd have better success arguing with a mountain than I would changing his mind.

Ms. Kwan and another detective came in carrying their forensics kits. She came over and grasped my hand. "They said on the radio you were here. You okay?"

"Sort of." I sucked in a shaky breath. "I'm mostly just worried about my Mom now."

She nodded, and then she and the other detective began to carefully go over the cabin for evidence.

Wire pulled up in his old Jeep, bringing Sean, Maeve, and Lupe with him. I noticed we were missing just one member of the club. As she entered, Lupe looked at me with sympathetic eyes but she didn't say anything. Maeve and Wire wanted to know what happened; I told them briefly what had transpired.

"You did a heck of a job," Maeve told me. I wasn't sure if it was a compliment or sarcasm.

"I told you not to do anything stupid," Wire chided me. "You're gonna get CSC shut down now, for sure."

I didn't know what to say. He was probably right, but what could I have done differently? It was my mom, after all. I couldn't have just stood there and done nothing.

Ms. Kwan was looking at us, and I thought maybe she wanted to say something in reply to Wire's remark. Instead, she turned her attention back to the scene.

"We have too many workers in here," she said. "This is a small area, and there may be clues vital to finding Ken's mother. So everyone stay toward the perimeters. Don't move unless I tell you to. Don't touch anything—not even the walls or furniture. If you do need to handle something, use gloves and tweezers. These are critical minutes for this case and we don't want to mess it up." She divided up the small building with an imaginary grid, then assigned a square to each detective. Sean and Maeve each got a square to search as well. Then Ms. Kwan gave Lupe her camera and told her to take pictures.

"Look at this!" Sean held up a silver and corral earring with a pair of tweezers.

"The lady in red was wearing one like that!" I exclaimed. It was one of the items on the mental list I'd made.

"Nice clip-ons," Ms. Kwan noted as she took the earrings and placed them carefully in an evidence bag.

Through the window, I could see the pulsing lights of an approaching ambulance, shining on the wet window to create an eerie light show. "Dad says I have to go to the hospital," I told Detective Kwan, "but you have to make a computer sketch of that woman before I go." I felt a pang inside me, as though Jessa's absence had poked my heart with something sharp. She wouldn't be the one drawing the picture after all.

"If you don't take care of that bump on your head, you won't be able to help anyone," Ms. Kwan snapped. Then her face softened. "I promise you, Ken, everyone on the case will do our best to find your mom. We won't waste a minute. Soon as I'm done here, I'll come over to the hospital and bring Wire along to help on the art. Okay? But you need to get your head looked at now."

An EMT opened the door, letting a blast of cold, wet air in. "Watch out," Ms. Kwan warned him. "Mud on your boots could contaminate this crime scene."

The medical technician asked me from outside the threshold, "You need help getting to the ambulance?"

I shook my head and tiptoed across the cabin floor.

"Let me take your arm, just in case. It's slippery out here."

I said goodbye to my dad, the detectives, and the CSC crew. I hated leaving.

By the time Ms. Kwan and Wire arrived at Flagstaff Medical Center, it was nearly midnight. I had been admitted, given a room, and X-rayed, but I was still waiting for the results. My dad had stopped by, but he had gone again. As much as I'd kind of liked him to stay with me, I wanted him out looking for my mother more.

"Have they found her?" I asked Ms. Kwan.

She shook her head, and my heart dropped. "I'm afraid not, Ken. The storm makes it hard to see. We've put in a request for the Shadow Wolves special tracking unit from the Tohono O'Odham Nation to send someone up and help us. It's unusual, but given the urgency of our situation. . ."

I took a breath, tried to be brave. "It means a lot, knowing you're putting in special effort."

"We also requested a helicopter from the forest service, soon as the storm is clear. We should be able to get a team in the air tomorrow morning."

"Now," Wire said, pulling a laptop computer out of his satchel and flipping it open, "let's put a face on this mystery woman."

"I can help with that," said a familiar voice.

There, framed in the doorway, stood Jessa, her long blond dreadlocks dripping onto the floor, a soaking windbreaker clinging to her shoulders, and a bicycle helmet dangling from her hand.

"You biked all the way here in the storm?" I asked her.

"Ms. Kwan called and told me about your mom. Don't think I've forgiven you—not even for a moment—but it's a truce until we rescue your mother."

At least I knew where I stood with Jessa.

She sat next to Detective Kwan, who handed her a sketch pad and a couple of pencils. Then, for the next hour, I described as best I could the appearance of the woman at the cabin. Wire would ask, "Like this?" as he kept tapping in combinations, and Jessa quickly wore out the erasers on her pencils removing lines and features.

Finally, I looked at Jessa's picture and said, "That looks like her. So does the computer image. You've both got it."

"I'll have both pictures transmitted to all media outlets immediately," Detective Kwan promised as she got to her feet. "Ken, I'll call and check on your condition first thing in the morning. Assuming you're good to go, I'll ask the charter school's permission to let Crime Scene Club meet at my office in the Department. I'm sure, under the circumstances, they'll consider it part of your ongoing education in crime work—and I need all your help."

I heard Wire say to Jessa, "I can put your bike in back of the Jeep and drive you home."

"Thanks." Jessa turned toward the door, then looked back at me. "I'll send all my good thoughts toward your mom."

"Lupe says she's going to St. Mary's before school in the morning and spending her allowance to light all the prayer candles in the church," Detective Kwan added. "She wanted me to let you know."

"Mom needs all the help she can get," I told them. "Thanks again."

I didn't think I'd be able to sleep, not as nervous as I was about my mom, but no sooner had they all walked out the door than I lay my throbbing head on the pillow and fell into exhausted sleep.

Chapter 7
THE PROOF IS IN THE EARRING

I woke early the next morning; my anxious mind would not allow me more rest, and the nurse waking me every few hours to check my vital signs didn't help. The doctor made his rounds before seven; he told me the X-rays gave no cause for alarm, and I would be released within the hour.

I was wishing for some fresh clothes and a toothbrush, when Dad walked in the door holding a duffel bag filled with just those things. Now that he was no longer worried about my health, he didn't waste time getting to what was on his mind. "That was beyond stupid what you did last night, you know that."

I nodded.

"I was going ape worrying about you this weekend."

"I'm sorry," I said.

Dad looked at me with this funny expression I wasn't sure I'd ever seen before. He clenched and unclenched his fists. "Thinking it over," he said, "I would have done the same thing, at your age, under those circumstances." His stone-hard face looked just a little softer, and he slapped a hand on my back. "Get dressed, kid. Time for action."

That's the closest thing to approval I've ever heard from him.

I had just finished changing when Mr. Chesterton came in the room. He gave my hand a bone-crushing squeeze and then explained that Ms. Kwan had called him this morning to tell him about my mother's plight. "The state, county, local PD, and CSC are all working together to find your mother. Our club is meeting in less than an hour at Ms. Kwan's office."

He was still speaking when two more people came in: Sean had driven my truck from the cabin, and he and Maeve were here to take me to the meeting.

"Let's get out of here," Maeve urged. "Last time I was in this hospital Kevin Brown tried to choke me to death. The place still creeps me out."

"Yeah," Sean said, "but then someone came with a nice vase full of flowers."

"Black dahlias, so appropriate." They smiled at each other.

A nurse stuck her head in, "Hey, this room is getting crowded."

"Guess we better go," I said.

A short time later, all the members of Crime Scene Club, along with Mr. Chesterton and Ms. Kwan, were gathered in her office. I noticed Ms. Kwan had bags under her eyes, and her clothes were a bit crumpled. She's normally meticulous about her appearance, so I had to think she was awake all night working on the case.

The detective brought us up to speed. "Still no sign of the kidnappers. We followed the tracks for both vehicles in the mud—a blind man could have done that—but when they left the dirt roads and got back onto the pavement, their trail disappeared. We're guessing they went a ways on the main road, then back into the forest. There are hundreds of miles of back-country roads. A skilled tracker will be up from Tucson and head for the woods shortly, and the winds have died down enough that forest service will have a chopper in the air within the hour."

"What about evidence from the cabin? Anything that'll help?" Wire asked.

"Sketches of the woman based on Ken's testimony are already being shown on the TV news and Internet, as well as a special insert in today's paper. I submitted the earring we found to the Northern Arizona University DNA lab. We'll get a profile from them and run it through the FBI's Combined DNA Index System, to see if it matches any known criminals' DNA fingerprint. We should have results from that within the hour."

"I might have something useful," Lupe volunteered. "It may be nothing, but. . ."

"Any clue could be helpful at this point," Mr. Chesterton encouraged her. "What have you found?"

"I couldn't sleep last night, so I searched all the news stories and related items on the Internet. I know it sounds funny, but sometimes overlooked information—even facts that are public knowledge—can be useful."

"So are you going to tell us?" Maeve sounded impatient.

"At the museum, when we all gathered for the exhibition, their curator was talking about the baskets, and I distinctly heard him say their collection was worth half a million."

Heads nodded; we all recalled the same thing.

"In yesterday's paper there was a follow-up article on the theft. It said that NMM has submitted a claim for $1.2 million for the stolen artifacts."

Sean whistled. "That's more than twice the amount he mentioned in the speech."

"Like I said, it may be nothing. . ."

"But it could point to a motive for the theft," Wire remarked. "If it was an inside job, someone in the museum could over-charge insurance. Maybe an employee with access to the museum's bank accounts is writing checks for their own use."

"I looked into the museum's financial records," Lupe added. "They haven't been doing well lately. All the staff took a pay cut last year, and this insurance settlement would be more than their annual operating budget."

"The woman at the cabin paid a quarter of a million for the stolen items," I put in. "It would be worth that to hire a thief to steal the artifacts—then make almost a million off insurance for their replacement."

"Would one of you like to run over to the museum and see if anyone there knows our mysterious lady in red?" Mr. Chesterton suggested.

"I'll go," I offered, itching to do something.

"Me too." Wire grabbed a copy of Jessa's portrayal of the woman.

"Phone us immediately if you find something," Detective Kwan admonished.

"That was a waste of time," I told Wire, half an hour later. Our questioning of workers at the Northern Mountain Museum had produced no leads. Several of the staff said, "She looks kind-of like someone I know," but no one could give a definite match to the picture. Meanwhile, I knew that with every hour that passed, Mom's life was in worse danger. Everyone had worked hard—and I appreciated it— but time was running out.

"Just a minute, got a call coming in." Wire pointed to the Bluetooth in his ear. He stood motionless for a minute, saying, "uh-huh," and "really?" and "no kidding?" Then he turned to me. "This gets weirder by the minute."

"What?"

"That earring Sean found in the cabin?"

"Yeah?"

"Are you sure the woman was wearing it?"

"Positive."

"You got your cranium pretty rattled. Sure you aren't confusing things?"

"Yes, I'm sure! Why?"

"The DNA lab got results back. We don't have a match on the CODIS base, but that's male DNA on the earring."

"She's a he?"

"Seems so. Wanna make some changes to our sketch of the suspect?"

We climbed into Wire's jeep. He opened up a laptop and clicked onto the Ident-a-Criminal system.

"Let's do away with that long blond hair," I suggested. "Go for a short-cut, nondescript male haircut instead."

The image changed dramatically.

"Now off with the lipstick and eye shadow." Wire was tapping away on the keyboard.

We both stared at the face.

"He looks familiar now, but I still can't place him," Wire said.

Then it hit me. "Add eyeglasses."

"Like this?"

"No. Make them square."

"These?"

"Widen the frames, and darken them."

"Would you look at that! It's Dr. Hemmer, the curator."

"Quick," I said, "back to the museum!"

Chapter 8
TWO SMOKING BARRELS

We ran to the information desk. "Is the curator in?" I gasped.

"Dr. Hemmer?" The woman behind the desk looked up at us. "He's about to leave for an archaeological expedition to the Andes. It's a wonderful opportunity that just came up."

"Yeah." Cynicism dripped from Wire's voice. "Wonderful opportunity. Very convenient."

"So, he's gone already?" I asked, fearing the worst.

"Funny you should ask, he's going to fly out this afternoon, but I just saw him stop into the warehouse. He said he wanted to examine a few artifacts before his trip."

"Where's the warehouse?"

"Out back through that door, but it's only open for museum employees. . ."

I was already dashing toward the exit she had indicated.

"Hold up!" Wire shouted, "Rules, remember? We're supposed to call CSC."

I threw him my cell phone. "Speed dial number one," I shouted and kept running.

I was now behind the museum proper, facing a very large building with a small open door. I stepped inside, and for a few moments, until my eyes adjusted to the darkness, I could see absolutely nothing. I breathed in a musty smell, and as my pupils widened, I saw row upon row of enormous shelves, from back to front and ceiling to floor of the large building. A stuffed grizzly bear reared up from the shadows, its long claws extended toward me. On one wall, a set of Polynesian masks glared down at me with bulging eyes, extended tongues, and pointed teeth.

I crept forward, down an aisle flanked by fossilized bones on one side and dusty mannequins on the other. For a minute, I wondered if the woman at the desk was mistaken about the curator being here; the lights were off, no one else seemed to be in here. Then I noticed a faint illumination at the end of the row.

On tip-toe, like a shadow, I moved closer. In the glow of a flashlight beam I saw a now-familiar face. He was pulling objects out of a box: strands of glistening silver Native jewelry; an enormous squash-blossom necklace; an intricately formed Zuni pendant. Those artifacts must have been worth thousands.

"Items for your personal collection? Or do they go to the black market after you flee the country?" I asked.

He jumped at the sound of my voice, stared at me a moment, then turned and strode quickly down the row of stored artifacts, shining the flashlight beam toward a shelf. I saw, for just an instant, the glint of old steel: a double-barreled shotgun. He dropped the flashlight and reached toward the shelf. That thing can't be loaded, I thought, but he grabbed the antique weapon and swung it toward me.

I leaped, kicking in the darkness toward the barrel of the gun.

Wham!

The blast echoed off musty relics and old brick walls. Lead shot spattered the room. Guess I was wrong about the thing not being loaded.

I spun around again and managed to clasp the stock of the gun. Dr. Hemmer and I struggled in the dark.

"I should have killed you when I had the chance!" He spat the words; I could feel his saliva hit my face. Anger surged through my limbs, and I yanked harder on the shotgun.

Wham!

The second shot was deafening. It hit the huge stuffed bear in its midsection, blowing out a chunk several feet wide. The grizzly's top half fell forward, its enormous claws and fangs crashing down on us.

Under a pile of mothball-smelling fur, claws, and teeth, I wrenched the gun out of the man's hands and smashed the butt into his chest. He coughed, swore; punched me hard in the nose.

And then the lights came on. A museum security guard came rushing down the aisle, pistol drawn. "What's going on here?"

"This punk attacked me," Hemmer shouted. "He tried to kill me with this old shotgun. He must be one of the thieves who stole our artifacts. Arrest him."

"He's lying," I gasped. "He's the thief! He hired criminals to steal the baskets so he could profit from the insurance money."

The curator chuckled. "What an imagination!" He looked at the guard, "Are you going to stand there, or are you going to do your job?"

"Don't move, kid." The security man whipped out a pair of handcuffs and snapped them on me.

"But I'm with Crime Scene Club, we're working with the police, I'm trying to save my mother."

The guard rolled his eyes. "Are you hurt, Dr. Hemmer?"

"This hoodlum may have broken a rib. Thank heavens you came when you did."

Wire rushed in the door, followed by the woman from the security desk. "Whoa there, you're arresting the wrong guy," Wire yelled.

"Who on earth are you?" The security guard had probably never seen so much excitement.

"He's obviously an accomplice of this teenage thug," the curator said. "Arrest him, too."

"Just a second," I begged the guard. "It will only take a moment to check a few facts. Have you seen the TV and papers today? The lady in red? That's your boss here—wearing a blond wig. Didn't she look familiar? Wire there has my cell phone. Dial one, it'll only take a moment. You'll get Detective Kwan of the Flag PD. She'll back our story."

I could almost see the wheels turning in the security guard's head. "Dr. Hemmer, I'm going to have to ask you to come with me for just a minute, sir."

The curator hesitated an instant, then bolted toward the door.

I was handcuffed, but I still had free movement of my legs. I stuck one foot out and he tripped, falling flat on his face in a collection of Kachina dolls and blankets.

Once the museum curator was arrested, it all went down like a house of cards. Sure enough, he had intended to flee the country and receive funds diverted to his bank from the insurance money, taking with him the stolen baskets—he had paid the thieves only a small fraction of their real value—and a number of other items he had "borrowed" from the museum warehouse. Charged with a pile of offenses, he was eager to bargain, so he gave the police a phone number he used to reach Rubio and Sandy. Officers set up a trap and apprehended the kidnappers. Thank heavens, Mom was unharmed.

Even before she was freed, the Flag PD had received a call from the FBI: Stella Benally was working undercover for the Federal Bureau of Investigation. They knew someone in the Southwest was stealing and selling high-end Native artifacts on the black market, and word was out that NMM's Apache basket collection would be the next likely target. Mom's expertise in Apache weaving and her job at the Bureau of Indian Affairs made her a

perfect undercover agent. Mom always seemed so normal; it never occurred to me that she could be a spy. She made a few shady contacts and was soon enlisted to help with the heist. Hector Rubio and Joe Sandy guessed her true role just before I busted into their cabin hideout.

I can't even tell you how happy I was when Mom stepped out of the officers' patrol car, ran to me, and hugged me.

"Mom, thank God you're okay." I was crying, but I didn't care who saw the tears.

She was crying too. "Ken, I'm so sorry. I've missed you so much these last years. I told myself I was better off avoiding your father—and that you were better off with him, not being torn between us. But I've missed years out of your life. And look what a wonderful young man you're turning out to be! I promise—if you give me another chance, we'll see a lot more of each other from now on."

Chapter 9
FORMING A TRUCE

Later that afternoon, I got a text message:

SECRET MEETING TONIGHT. CAFÉ PARAD-
ISO, 8PM. TELL NO ONE. WIRE.

When I arrived, Wire, Maeve, and Sean were already seated with empty cups of coffee in front of them.

"What's up, Wire?" I asked. "You find another hidden treasure?"

He chuckled, recalling our last secret meeting. "Nope. Treasure hunting is more trouble than it's worth. Let's wait for a few more members, then we'll talk."

Lupe and Jessa arrived together. Lupe works at this coffee shop as a barista, and Sunshine Daydream, the owner, had given the girls a ride into town.

"Free coffee for Lupe's friends," Sunshine offered, as she walked by our table.

"I suppose you wonder why I've called this meeting," Wire intoned in a mock self-important voice.

"Don't tell me: you're a taped message and we're Mission Impossible," I said.

"Or we're angels and you're Charlie?" Jessa smiled, but I noticed she didn't look my way.

"Jessa could be Farrah, Lupe maybe Jaclyn—but I am no way going to be Kate," Maeve retorted.

"You girls watch TV Land too much." Wire held up a finger. "First order of business: Sean has something from his aunt."

We turned toward him. Sean wasn't an official member of CSC, but he had become Maeve's sidekick—or boyfriend? No one was sure. And was useful having someone who lives under Ms. Kwan's roof hanging out with us.

"Aunt Dot wanted you all to see the official report for the PD on our latest case. I made copies." He handed them around. "She said, 'read it carefully and be familiar with it—just in case.'"

"In case?"

"You'll see."

We all sat quietly, reading through the report. It was very wordy and boring, but it was pretty much everything I knew already—but with a few certain details lacking. Like the fact that I failed to report my sighting of Mom and the criminals, and the fact that I confronted a wanted man and almost got my head bashed in at a convenience store, and the fact that I went after the bad guys all by myself ahead of the police—in short, all the things that would get me kicked out of CSC if they were reported.

It appears someone wants me to remain in the club. Or is she guarding the club itself?

"Tell Ms. Kwan she did a great job with the report," I told Sean.

He grinned. "Thought you'd like it."

"Second order of business," Wire said, "is more difficult. We may have the best crime fighting unit in Northern Arizona, right at this table." He gestured at all of us.

"Isn't that a little arrogant?" Lupe asked.

"Not really. I've noted the time it took us to solve three major crimes and compared that with the effectiveness of your average U.S. detective department—we're way ahead of the curve in closing cases. However," he frowned, "we can't continue effectively when three of our members"—he stared at me, Lupe, and Jessa—"aren't talking to each other."

"Major crap went down," Jessa said, "but I didn't start it."

I took a long breath, closed my eyes, and forced words out: "It's my fault. I'm a real jerk."

"Wow," Wire said, "I don't think I've ever heard you talk like that, Ken. Kind of refreshing."

Lupe was looking at Jessa. "I knew what Ken and did I was wrong, but I didn't mean to hurt you, Jessa. I wish it never happened."

"All right," Maeve said. "Confession is good for the soul, but let's get on to the point. What happened, happened. Mr. Wonderful here"—she waved a black-tipped hand at me—"totally messed up, but he's not the first or the last guy to do that. Now, we have to figure out a way to make this club work from this point on."

My mind was scrambling, like a squirrel darting back and forth in the middle of the road just about to get plastered by a car. If the squirrel doesn't choose one direction and stick with it, he's road kill. All right, I told myself, make up your mind! Choose Jessa? Choose Lupe? How? What to say?

I took a gulp of air. "Jessa, I'm sorry, more sorry than I can ever tell you—I never should have cheated. Can we please start over and I swear I'll never look at another girl again."

I could see the pain in Lupe's eyes.

Jessa took a deep breath; there was a strange look on her face. She turned slowly toward me. "Ken, when we broke up I lost my best friend."

I nodded. "I lost mine, too."

"Looking back, maybe part of it was my fault. Maybe I was too possessive." She paused, searching for words. "So here's what I'm going to do, I'm going to be your friend. I'll talk to you, and we'll cooperate on CSC cases. But we're just going to be friends—okay? Hands to yourself, don't presume too much, and we're both free to date whomever we want."

This wasn't exactly what I wanted to hear.

"And another thing," she added. "Red, White, and Blues sounds awful without me, so I'm going to sing with the band again."

"We are the worst without you," I agreed. "We'll all be glad to have you back."

Then Lupe spoke, her voice shaky. "I'm willing to be friends with both of you, at least I'll try. But Ken, don't ever take advantage of me again."

I felt sick inside. I wanted to tell her she meant so much to me, but there are some things that can just never be expressed quite right. If I tried to straighten things with Lupe, Jessa might take back the "friends" part. I had made my choice, and this was the outcome. I nodded.

Not much hope for a future relationship with Lupe, and as for Jessa, we're now "just friends." I blew it, all right. I've seen these "let's just be friends" scenarios after couples break up. But I'm willing to give it a try, because it beats not talking. And who knows what could happen in the future?

Maeve gave a Cheshire cat smile. "Well, I'm glad that's settled. Let's all give the secret CSC handshake and everything's good."

Jessa's nose wrinkled. "Uh, I didn't know we have a handshake."

"Oh, yes. That's our final order of business." Wire chuckled. "Anyone want more coffee while we talk about it?"

I leaned back in my chair, taking stock of things. Mom is back in my life again, and maybe, just maybe, Dad and I might get along better in the future. The girls and I are talking. So all that's an improvement—I think. I doubt I'll be as popular at school as I was before this mess began, but that might be good: maybe I can be more real with people now. I'll be ready to get up tomorrow and face another day.

I just hope Coyote doesn't cross my path again any time soon.

FORENSIC NOTES

CRIME SCENE CLUB, CASE #3

CHAPTER 1

Evidence List

Vocab Words

traditional
prestigious
conundrum
liaison
faux
heritage
elite
curator
sacredness
functional
theatrical

Deciphering the Evidence

Ken explains to Jessa that his mom is connected to *traditional* Jicarella Apache ways, meaning that she remains true to its customs and beliefs.

Mr. C is pleased to announce that an institution as esteemed and reputable as the *prestigious* Heard Museum has agreed to lend the Northern Mountain Museum some of its pieces.

Ken's *conundrum* of not being able to decide between the two girls in his life is a problem many teenage boys might not mind having.

As a *liaison* between the local police department and Crime Scene Club, Detective Kwan acts as the communication link between the world of law enforcement and the teenagers who are learning about it.

Faux torches in the meeting room at the Northern Mountain Museum suggest to Ken that someone was trying to create an artificial mood of mystery and drama.

Ken wonders why the European-American *elite*, who historically have used their powerful and influential status to suppress the *heritage* of Native Americans, have taken an interest in the traditions and beliefs passed down from his ancestors in the form of Indian art.

As the person in charge of the museum, the *curator* is responsible for opening the exhibit with a speech.

Native people of the Southwest believed practical objects were holy connections to the spiritual world and making them beautiful was a way of expressing this "everyday *sacredness*."

The *functional* vessels made by early Native Americans were useful and practical but came to be appreciated by later generations as decorative art.

Before unveiling the masterpieces of traditional Apache art, the curator points to the covered cases with a *theatrical* gesture in order to create a *dramatic* sense of anticipation.

The World of Forensics

Our English word "forensic" comes from the Latin word forensis, which means "forum"—the public area where in the days of ancient Rome a person charged with a crime presented his case. Both the person accused of the crime and the accuser would give speeches presenting their sides of the story. The person with the best forensic skills usually won the case.

In the modern world, "forensics" has come to mean the various procedures, many of them scientific in nature, used to answer questions of interest to the legal system—usually, to solve a crime. Detective Kwan and the members of the CSC use many of these procedures in their cases. In this case, their third, the procedures involved with forensic art are particularly useful to them.

Forensic Procedures Used in CSC Case #3

Forensic Art

Forensic art refers to the creation of visual images by hand or computer to identify

Who Are the Jicarilla Apache, the Diné, and the Pueblo?

The Jicarilla Apache are one of seven southern Athabascan groups who migrated out of Canada to the American southwest sometime between A.D. 1300 and 1500. They settled in an area of more than 50 million acres in northern New Mexico, southern Colorado, and western Oklahoma. *Jicarilla* (pronounced "hee-kuh-ree-uh") is the Mexican-Spanish word for "little basket," and the Jicarilla Apache are acclaimed for their beautiful handcrafted baskets.

Diné is another word for the Navajo people, the largest Native American tribe in North America. *Diné* means "the people" in the Navajo language, and is the term that members traditionally use for themselves.

The Pueblo people are a Native American people living mainly in New Mexico and Arizona. Spanish explorers who encountered them in the sixteenth century called the towns they were living in "pueblos," which was the Spanish word for "villages."

Who Is Pelé?

Pelé is widely regarded as one of the best soccer players of all time. He is considered a national hero in his native country of Brazil.

What Is Navajo Nation?

The Navajo Nation is a Native American homeland covering 17 million acres of northeastern Arizona, as well as parts of Utah and New Mexico. It is the largest land area under Native American jurisdiction in the United States.

perpetrators and victims of crime. Jessa, Wire, and Maeve argue over the merits of a human artist versus a computer program for creating a visual representation of a person based on interviews. Some sketch artists go to great lengths to consider the emotions of the witness or victim. Trying to recall specific details under pressure can be stressful, so putting the person at ease can help him or her to provide more useful information. A human artist also may have sophisticated knowledge of facial anatomy and the spacing of features that allows a more accurate portrait to be drawn. Witnesses and victims may struggle with trying to re-create a face from random features pulled up on a computer program, because humans tend to view faces as a whole, rather than as a collection of features. For this reason, some computer simulation software can show a whole face that matches the description in a general way, and then the features can be fine-tuned according to what doesn't look quite right. A computer program makes it easy to change hairstyles or eye color, or add or subtract identifying details, such as glasses or a beard. Wire does this with Jessa's sketch of the lady in red from the cabin, using his computer to make the portrait less feminine so that it quickly becomes clear that the "woman" is actually Dr. Hemmer.

Forensic art doesn't have to be created in just two dimensions. Some forensic artists create three-dimensional sculptures of crime victims from skulls. They often work together with scientists so that the details of facial muscles, soft tissue, and other elements of the head and face are accurate and realistic.

Skilled forensic artists combine a knowledge of human anatomy and psychology with technical artistic ability to assist law enforcement personnel with solving mysteries and bringing perpetrators to justice.

What Is a Kachina?

A Kachina is an ancestral spirit of the Pueblo people. *Kachina* means "life bringer" in the Hopi language, and according to the Hopi Pueblo, the Kachinas visit their villages after the winter solstice to make the world new again. *Kachina* can refer to the spirits, the dancers who embody the spirits during religious ceremonies, or the carved dolls that are presented to children to teach them about the spirits.

What Is Art Deco?

Art deco refers to a style of art that was popular in the 1920s and 1930s. The term art deco comes from the name of an exposition held in Paris in 1925 celebrating "arts décoratifs et industriels modernes" or "modern industrial and decorative art." The art deco movement was influenced by modern advances in technology, as can be seen in its dramatic use of geometric shapes and stylish and elegant designs. When Ken refers to "someone's art deco notion of Pueblo art" he is implying that the art has been modernized and is therefore not authentic Pueblo art.

CHAPTER 2

Evidence List

Vocab Words

personification
profilers
fence
credible
essence
anonymous
warrants
angst
crescendo

Deciphering the Evidence

Ken thinks that in his dad's mind, his mom became the *personification* of evil after she left them; to his dad, she represents an idea in human form, in this case the idea of evil.

Ken's dad compares forensic artists to criminal *profilers*, professionals who try to identify perpetrators by analyzing the way they committed the crime and what this might say about their personality and lifestyle.

Detective Kwan suspects that whoever stole the artifacts did it to *fence* the stolen goods, or sell the stolen property later. The word *fence* was first used in this way around 1700 by thieves who stole and then sold items under "*defense* of secrecy."

Detective Kwan doubts that Maeve would be *credible*, or believable, in the Native art scene.

Detective Kwan says that the best forensic artists capture the inner *essence*, or the most important, truest nature of a perpetrator.

The woman whose identity is not known is referred to by Detective Kwan as the "*anonymous* woman."

The two men on the surveillance tape have outstanding *warrants*: official orders to either arrest them or search their property for evidence of criminal behavior.

Jessa expresses anger and *angst*, or emotional turmoil, when she sings "Piece of My Heart."

Sticks brought the song to a crashing *crescendo*, intensifying the force of his drumming to match Jessa's powerful singing.

Forensic Procedures Used in CSC Case #3

Trace Evidence

At the scene of the crime, police officers search for "physical traces": spilled fluids, drops of blood, strands of fiber. They know that every person who is physically involved in a crime always—no matter how careful he or she may be—leaves some tiny trace behind; he or she often takes something away as well. Seemingly insignificant things—tiny threads, hairs, dust, pollen, bits of metal and glass—can make all the difference when it comes to solving a crime.

Trace evidence usually isn't enough to build an entire case against a suspect—but it can be very useful to detectives nevertheless, giving them important clues that may help them look in the right direction for a culprit or confirm other evidence.

Hair samples in this case can be compared with the hair of the suspects once they are in custody. If enough properties are similar so that the sample is consistent with the suspects' hair, the hair samples can be used as evidence, although not as definite proof of their guilt. Hair analysis can tell things such as whether the hair came from a human or an animal, whether it came from someone of a particular race, and whether the hair has been dyed, cut in a particular way, or pulled out. If a hair shaft with its follicle has been found, it may be possible to determine the blood type or DNA of the person it came from.

Fingerprints

Fingerprints have been of interest to humans for various reasons for much of our history: the handprints left behind on the walls of caves suggest that these marks were important to our earliest ancestors. In terms of criminal investigations, in first-century Rome, a palm print was used to frame someone for murder. In the 1800s, fingerprinting replaced a more cumbersome way of identifying criminals that involved taking as many as fourteen different measurements of the criminal's body. Once scientists realized that everyone's fingerprints are unique and don't change over time, fingerprinting became the preferred method for identifying individuals.

There are three basic types of fingerprints: visible prints, such as those made in ink, paint, or blood; invisible, or latent, prints, which can only be seen using certain techniques; and plastic prints, which are made by touching something soft, such as wax. A fingerprint can be made even when there are no substances such as paint or soft wax simply from sweat mixed with the body's amino acids. Amazingly, scientists have developed ways to lift fingerprints off human skin.

Investigators must make invisible prints visible, and they have many ways of doing this. A common method is to brush a fine powder on the print and blow off the excess. The powder that remains leaves a clear impression of the print that can then be photographed and lifted with tape, which is then preserved on a special card. Prints can also be developed with chemicals, digital imaging, dyes, and fumes.

Detective Kwan notes a common problem in criminal cases—when only partial prints are found. Some law enforcement officials will not bother dusting partial prints, because they believe they cannot make a positive identification with them, and they are often not admissible as evidence in court. However, new software is being developed to enhance partial or hard-to-see fingerprints, and it is being used to identify and convict perpetrators. The software doesn't change the print, but clarifies it if it is difficult to see—for example, if it's on patterned wallpaper.

When Detective Kwan indicates that the partial fingerprints are not good enough

2.1 Developments in non-invasive fingerprint recovery techniques, such as chemical and digital imaging methods, have been promising. These methods can potentially salvage fingerprints even after they have been removed.

to be matched on the national fingerprint registry, she is referring to the Integrated Automated Fingerprint Identification System (IAFIS), which is maintained by the FBI. This system matches an unknown print against prints of identified individuals. In less than one second, the computer can compare a set of ten fingerprints against a half million prints. A list of prints that closely match pops up, and then a technician does the final analysis.

Surveillance Tapes

The use of surveillance tapes is another important strategy for solving crimes. Advances in video technology have made it possible to more effectively identify criminals in action. Computer-based video enhancement systems can be used to turn dark, shaky, blurry images into clearer, more stable ones. If an image is grainy, as in the case of the surveillance tape supplied by the clerk at Mountain View Convenience Store, video enhancement technology such as that used by Detective Kwan can be used to sharpen the image.

Mug Shot Databases

Detective Kwan was able to match the pictures of the suspects with an online database of criminal mug shots. A mug shot database provides law enforcement with pictures of all individuals who have been

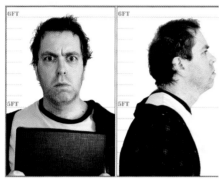

2.2 Facial images are crucial for criminal identification. Advancements in computer assisted facial recognition technology could enable scientists to make accurate facial comparisons between mug shots and surveillance images.

arrested. Victims or investigators can then use these pictures for identification.

> ### Fast Fact
> The term *mug* is believed to have come either from the slang word for *face* or from the sense of mug as in "grimace." Early subjects would twist their faces up, or grimace, to make their photographs less useful for identification.

Warrants

In the United States (as well as in many other countries, including Canada and the United Kingdom), certain citizen rights are legally protected. In the United States, these rights are guaranteed by the Constitution and the Bill of Rights. A warrant, however, allows police to cross these legal lines.

113

A warrant is an authorization written by an officer of the court (usually a judge), which commands an otherwise illegal act that would violate individual rights; it grants the person who carries out the warrant protection from any legal damages. The most common warrants are search warrants (which give the police permission to search someone's private property when there is reason to believe that evidence connected to a crime will be found there), arrest warrants (when police bring a suspect into custody until a court officer determines what happens next), and execution warrants (when a convicted person receives a death sentence).

A typical arrest warrant in the United States, such as the ones Detective Kwan is discussing in this chapter, would be worded something like this:

> This Court orders the Sheriff or Constable to find the named person, wherever he or she may be found, and deliver said person to the custody of the Court.

CHAPTER 3

Evidence List

Vocab Words

expertise
alleged

Deciphering the Evidence

When Ken's dad called the man his mom was living with, he was told she was out of town on business related to her *expertise* in basketry. Expertise is skill or knowledge in a particular area.

Ken dreaded the thought of performing in front of people who knew he was the son of an *alleged* criminal. His mother was suspected of being a criminal, although she was not proven to be one yet.

Forensic Procedures Used in CSC Case #3

Call-In Leads

Call-in leads can be an effective way for law enforcement officials to involve the public in helping track down a perpetrator. Someone may know or have seen the suspect, and the information he or she provides could turn the investigators' attention in a

115

new direction, bringing them closer to finding the person responsible for the crime. Generally the tip line for calling in guarantees anonymity, meaning callers are not required to identify themselves, in case they are reluctant or afraid to get involved. Sometimes a reward for information is offered as well, as an incentive to encourage people to call. Officials cannot know if a lead will lead them to important information until they follow it, so in most cases, every lead is investigated. They may need to investigate hundreds of leads before one of them turns out to provide truly useful information.

Role of the Media

The local news program KFLG broadcasts information about the three people wanted for questioning in the theft of artifacts from the Northern Mountain Museum. The media play an important role alongside law enforcement in helping to prevent and solve crimes. Publicizing details of a crime, such as photographs or sketches of the suspects, surveillance tapes, or even just descriptions of the perpetrators may lead someone to come forward with useful information. News outlets can post a phone number provided by investigators for the public to call with any leads they may have.

CHAPTER 4

Evidence List

Vocab Words

emancipated minor
claustrophobic
RPG
dispatcher

Deciphering the Evidence

Wire lives by himself in his trailer because
he is an *emancipated minor*. He has been
granted certain legal rights of adulthood—
in this case, the right to live without the
supervision of parents or guardians—even
though he is not yet an adult by the standards of the law.

Wire's small trailer filled with electronics
equipment feels *claustrophobic* to Ken; it
gives him an uncomfortable feeling of being
closed in.

Wire compares cracking crime cases to
RPGs, or role-playing games, in which
participants take on the roles of fictional
characters, often in a battle of good guys
against bad guys.

Wire and Ken hear a police *dispatcher* relaying a sighting of the suspects. The dis-

117

patcher is the person or team who relay calls related to law enforcement activities so that the appropriate response to public safety matters can be coordinated.

Forensic Procedures Used in CSC Case #3

Satellite Images

Wire has the equipment in his trailer to call up a satellite image of the area where the suspects have been sighted. He is even able to identify the only dwelling in the area, allowing him to pinpoint a possible destination for the suspects.

Images broadcast by satellites have more commonly been used by the military for intelligence surveillance than by law enforcement officials for fighting crime. But advances in satellite technology have provided more precise images that could be used to reconstruct the scene of a crime or accident. New satellites have been able to show objects as small as three feet wide. Consider the fact that an object as small as a car can be seen in a driveway. If a suspect states that he was home at the time a crime was committed but the satellite image shows an empty driveway at that time, this information could possibly be used as evidence in court.

It is now possible for you to view many satellite images from your home computer using Web sites on the Internet such as Google Earth. This is most likely how Wire was able to call up a satellite image on his computer. Once you find a site with this capability, simply type in your address, for example, and you can zoom in on a picture of your street and even of your house, right down to the car in your own driveway!

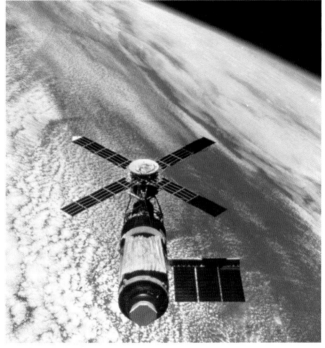

4.1 The use of satellite imagery to support forensic cases is controversial, but steadily Expanding. FBI investigators have sought the expertise of NASA scientists and their satellite imagery equipment to analyze criminal cases.

CHAPTER 5

Evidence List

Vocab Words

compliant

Deciphering the Evidence

Ken remembers that his mother seemed *compliant* the first time he saw her with the two men at Scorsese's. She appeared willing to be with her companions at the pizza parlor.

Forensic Procedures Used in CSC Case #3

Hostage Situation Tactics

The two male suspects have Ken's mother bound and gagged in the cabin they have retreated to in an effort to evade capture by the police. The two men are holding her against her will, and therefore she is a hostage rather than an accomplice.

Hostage-takers are not interested in the person they have taken hostage. They are after something, usually money, and they are using the hostage to get what they want from another party. They will make their demands known through a ransom note, phone call, or some other means of commu-

5.1 In this image, Sgt. Michael Walusz, an investigator with the U.S. Marine Corps Criminal Investigation Division, talks to a hostage taker from the command center during a simulated hostage situation.

nication, threatening the safety of the person they are holding captive if they don't get what they want in a certain time frame. In some cases, a person is kidnapped and "held for ransom." In other instances, a group of people is held against their will in an enclosed space, such as a bank or airplane, until the demands of their captors are met.

Law enforcement personnel must be prepared to deal with hostage-takers by knowing what works and what doesn't work in these tense situations. The primary goals are keeping the hostages safe and assuring their release. The negotiator should try to keep things calm and establish a relationship with the hostage-taker and between the hostage-taker and the hostages. In this way, the captor feels a connection to the person he or she is negotiating with as well as to the person or people being held, and may be more likely to cooperate and less likely to inflict harm.

CHAPTER 6

Evidence List

Vocab Words

transpired
perimeters

Deciphering the Evidence

After the incident at the cabin, Ken told Maeve and Wire what had *transpired*. In other words, he told them what had oc-curred.

Detective Kwan instructed everyone to stay toward the *perimeters*, or outer edges, of the cabin so as not to disturb any vital clues to finding Ken's mother.

Forensic Procedures Used in CSC Case #3

Forensic Kits

After the thieves flee the cabin, the detec-tives arrive on the scene carrying forensic kits. Once Detective Kwan has made sure that Ken is all right, she and the other de-tective use the tools in their kits to care-fully go over the cabin for evidence. Al-though there are probably thousands of different kinds of items that can be used in a forensic investigation, the detectives have

122

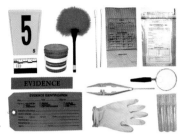

6.1 Crime scene investigators are equipped with a variety of tools to gather different types of physical evidence or to conduct on-site tests. Preservation of evidence is integral to criminal investigations.

likely brought with them some of the more common supplies that can be carried easily in a portable kit.

A basic forensic kit might include:

- chemical testing equipment for analyzing blood, drugs, gunshot residue (GSR), and explosives. Because these tests involve applying a chemical and looking for a color change, they are sometimes called color tests. Other terms used are screening tests and spot tests.

- swab collection kits, which can be used to collect cells from the inside of a subject's cheek for DNA analysis.

- equipment for collecting fingerprint evidence, including brushes, powders, lifting tape, and backing cards.

123

- evidence containers, for collecting evidence of all sizes. These containers can be plastic or paper bags, envelopes, jars, cans, or boxes. Some are specially made to hold sharp objects, such as needles or knives. Others are designed with special heat-sealed edges to prevent anyone from tampering with the evidence inside.

- safety supplies, such as protective clothing, masks, eyewear, gloves, cleaners and disinfectants, and biohazard disposal bags.

- tweezers, for picking up hair, fibers, or other small particles of evidence.

- gloves, to avoid contaminating the crime scene with fingerprints from members of the investigative team. Vinyl gloves may protect personnel from chemical or biological hazards, but some brands are thin enough to cause an impression to be left that could contaminate the crime scene. Because of this, it is recommended that either two pairs of gloves be worn, or that a pair of cotton gloves be worn underneath.

Avoiding Contamination of the Crime Scene

Contamination means to make something unclean or impure by having contact with it. In the context of a crime scene, contamination occurs when something interferes with the careful collection of evidence. Detective Kwan says that there are too many workers in the cabin and orders everyone to stay at the perimeters. If personnel are wandering all over the crime scene, touching surfaces, their footprints and fingerprints will mix with those of the individuals involved in the crime, making it more difficult to locate and analyze the prints of the perpetrators and victims. Thus, strict guidelines should be followed with regard to who is allowed in the area. The tools used by investigators in evidence collection, such as gloves, tweezers, and evidence bags, are all designed to prevent contamination. Trained personnel know the rules for collecting evidence, such as never putting suspect items and victim items in contact with one another. They also know the correct order for processing a crime scene. For example, trace evidence should be collected before fingerprinting to avoid contaminating the evidence with dusting powder.

Who Are the Shadow Wolves of the Tohono O' Odham Nation?

The Shadow Wolves are a special Native American law enforcement unit created by Congress in 1972. The U.S. government agreed to the demand of the Tohono O' Odham Nation that the officers of the unit have at least one-fourth Native American ancestry. They became the first federal law enforcement agents allowed to operate on Tohono land. Members of the Tohono O' Odham Nation reside mainly in the Sonoran Desert in the southwest United States and northwest Mexico.

CHAPTER 7

Evidence List

Vocab Words

meticulous
cranium

Deciphering the Evidence

Detective Kwan informed Mr. Chesterton of Ken's mother's *plight*. Plight refers to a difficult, dangerous, or unfortunate situation.

Ms. Kwan was normally *meticulous* in her appearance, so Ken guessed that she had been too busy working on the case all night to be concerned about details such as whether her clothes were wrinkled.

When Wire tells Ken that he got his *cranium* pretty rattled, he's referring to the part of the skull that encases the brain.

Forensic Procedures Used in CSC Case #3

DNA Testing

The members of Crime Scene Club learn from Detective Kwan that the earring found at the cabin has been submitted to a DNA lab. She explains that the profile provided by the lab will be run through the FBI's Combined DNA Index System, to see if it matches any known criminal's DNA finger-print.

DNA testing can be used for a number of purposes in forensic cases:

- to match a biological sample from the crime scene with a suspect.
- to clear criminals who are wrongly convicted of a crime.
- to solve a missing person case.
- to identify a victim who is not identifiable without DNA.

Sources of DNA that can be used as biological evidence include saliva, blood, semen, teeth, bones, hair, skin cells, and fingerprints.

7.1 Shown here is one method of collecting DNA samples: the cheek swab. In one of the early cases involving DNA testing, State vs. Wodall, Wodall was later exonerated of rape and robbery charges when DNA tests were conducted. Contrarily, in the case of Spencer vs. Commonwealth, DNA evidence upheld the conviction of Timothy Spencer who was convicted of rape and murder. (http://www.pbs.org/wgbh/pages/frontline/shows/case/revolution/wars.html)

The Combined DNA Index System (CODIS) is an electronic database of DNA profiles maintained by the FBI. Just as fingerprints found at a crime scene can be run through the Integrated Automated Fingerprint Identification System (IAFIS) to look for a match, DNA profiles from a crime scene can be entered into CODIS. This gives law enforcement personnel a way to identify suspects when no prior suspect exists.

The DNA database has four categories of DNA records:

- DNA records of persons convicted of crimes
- DNA samples taken from crime scenes
- DNA samples from unidentified human remains
- DNA samples voluntarily contributed from relatives of missing persons

CODIS produces a list of candidate matches. Only a qualified DNA Analyst can confirm or refute the match.

> ### Fast Fact
> With today's technology, it is possible to single out one person from all the people who have ever lived using DNA from a single hair root.

CHAPTER 8

Evidence List

Vocab Words

cynicism
squash-blossom necklace
black market

Deciphering the Evidence

Cynicism dripped from Wire's voice when he learned that Dr. Hemmer was about to leave the country on an expedition. He was distrustful of the motive behind the curator's trip because of what he had just seen on the Ident-A-Criminal system.

One of the objects Ken sees Dr. Hemmer pull out a box at the museum warehouse is a *squash-blossom necklace*. A squash-blossom necklace is a popular form of Native American art containing uniquely designed beads and a crescent-shaped pendant called a naja.

Ken asks Dr. Hemmer if the artifacts he is taking are for his personal collection or for the *black market*. Black market refers to the illegal business of buying and selling goods outside the control of government regulations.

Forensic Procedures Used in CSC Case #3

Undercover Work

Going undercover, the way Ken's mom does, is a procedure often used by police to infiltrate drug dealers and other criminal groups. Stella Benally's expertise in Apache weaving and her job at the Bureau of Indian Affairs made her an ideal FBI undercover agent for this case of stolen artifacts.

If this had been an actual case, she most likely would have worked for the FBI's Art Crime Team, which was established in 2004 to address art and cultural property crime cases.

The Art Crime Team's Senior Investigator, Robert Wittman, has been with the FBI

8.1 Since its establishment, the FBI Art Crime Team has recovered over $134 million dollars of cultural property items. (http://www.fbi.gov/hq/cid/arttheft/artcrimeteam.htm)

for 19 years and has recovered more than $215 million worth of stolen art and cultural property. He uses his training in art, antiques, jewelry, and gem identification to track down thieves around the world who steal from museums, galleries, and private art collections. Among his list of recovered items are Native American Apache medicine man Geronimo's eagle feathered war bonnet, which was valued at $1.2 million. He also reclaimed one of the original 14 copies of the Bill of Rights that had been stolen by a Union soldier during the Civil War. Wittman says that one of the main purposes of his work is to put something back in a museum or exhibit for the public to appreciate. He found it especially rewarding when the copy of the Bill of Rights was put on display and a thousand kids came to see it the first day.

Ken's mom "made a few shady contacts" to allow her to become part of the world where artifacts are stolen and sold on the black market. Robert Wittman does much the same thing in his real-life work as an investigator for the Art Crime Team. For example, in 2005, he arranged the purchase of a stolen Rembrandt self-portrait worth $36 million. Because of the use of undercover tactics, the sellers were not aware that a trap had been set for them. Once the sale was made, the sellers were arrested.

Robert Wittman still works as an undercover agent for the FBI, which is why, although his name appears in news stories, his photograph never does.

Who Are the Zuni?

The Zuni are a Native American tribe—one of the Pueblo peoples—who live mainly in western New Mexico. The Zuni have a unique language that is different than that of all the other Pueblo people. They also have a unique belief system that focuses on three deities, or gods: Earth Mother, Sun Father, and Moonlight-Giving Mother. The Sun in particular is worshipped—the Zuni words for daylight and life are the same. The making of traditional crafts, such as carved stone animals, jewelry, needlepoint, and pottery, is a big part of the Zuni culture.

CHAPTER 9

Wrapping Up the Case

This case involved hidden identities on both sides of the law. Stella Benally, Ken's mother, was an undercover agent who fooled the thieves into believing she wanted to help them steal the Native artifacts. Dr. Hemmer disguised himself as a woman so his true identity as curator of the museum would be protected while he was making a deal with the robbers. He might have gotten away with it if it weren't for some sharp thinking on the part of the Crime Scene Club members. Lupe knew that sometimes overlooked information can be useful: she noticed a discrepancy between the value Dr. Hemmer gave the artifact collection in his speech at the museum and the amount of the insurance claim the museum was submitting for the stolen artifacts as reported in a newspaper article. This led Wire to speculate that someone at the museum might be overcharging insurance. Another piece of the puzzle was added when DNA testing of the earring found in the cabin indicated that the DNA specimen from the earring was from a male, not a female. These are examples of how even a small bit of information can put investigators on the right track to solving a crime. It wasn't necessary to find an exact match for the DNA sample; even knowing that it came from a

man and not a woman was important information in this instance.

With Dr. Hemmer and the thieves in
police custody and Ken's mother safe, the
Crime Scene Club can consider the case
closed and relax for awhile as they wait to
see what their next assignment will be.

FURTHER READING

Boylan, Jeanne. *Portraits of Guilt: The Woman who Profiles the Faces of America's Deadliest Criminals.* New York: Pocket Boos, 2000.

Ferllini, Roxana. *Silent Witness. How Forensic Anthropology is Used to Solve the World's Toughest Crimes.* Buffalo, NY: Firefly Books, 2002.

Gibson, Lois. *Forensic Art Essentials: A Manual for Law Enforcement Artists.* Burlington, MA: Academic Press, 2008.

Innes, Brian. *Forensic Science.* Philadelphia, PA: Mason Crest Publishers, 2006.

Taylor, Karen T. *Forensic Art and Illustration.* Boca Raton: FL: CRC Press, 2001.

FOR MORE INFORMATION

American Academy of Forensic Sciences. www.aafs.org

Crime Library, "When Art Meets Crime," www.crimelibrary.com/criminal_mind/forensics/art/2.html

Federal Bureau of Investigation Art Theft Program, www.fbi.gov/hq/cid/arttheft/arttheft.htm

How Stuff Works, "How Crime Scene Investigation Works, www.howstuffworks.com/csi.htm

International Association for Identification. Forensic Artist Certification Process. www.theiai.org/certifications/artist/index.php

BIBLIOGRAPHY

Genge, N. E. *The Forensic Casebook.* New York: Ballantine Books, 2002.

Lyle, D.P. *Forensics for Dummies.* Indianapolis, IN: Wiley Publishing Inc., 2004

Michigan State Police. Forensic Art 101. www.michigan.gov/msp/0,1607,7-123-1589_3493_22454-59999--,00.html

Owen, David. *Hidden Evidence. Forty True Crimes and How Forensic Science Helped Solved Them.* Buffalo, NY: Firefly Books, 2000.

Ramsland, Katherine, "The Artist and the Murderer." http://www.trutv.com/library/crime/criminal_mind/forensics/art/8.html

Wecht, Cyril H. *Crime Scene Investigation.* Pleasantville, NY: The Reader's Digest Association, Inc., 2004.

INDEX

PICTURE CREDITS

Istock.com
    Alms, Brandon: p. 111, 123
    Brandenburg, Dan: p. 131
    Chesson, Kevin: p. 128
    Knallay, Kevin M.: p. 121
    Tippler, Niilo: p. 113

Jupiter Images: pp. 119

United States Marine Corps

To the best knowledge of the publisher, all images not spe-
cifically credited are in the public domain. If any image has
been inadvertently uncredited, please notify Harding House
Publishing Service, Vestal, New York 13850, so that credit can
be given in future printings.

BIOGRAPHIES

Author

Kenneth McIntosh is a freelance writer and college instructor who lives in beautiful Flagstaff, Arizona (while CSC is fictional, Flagstaff is definitely real). He has enjoyed crime fiction—from Sherlock Holmes to CSI and Bones—and is thankful for the opportunity to create his own detective stories. Now, if he could only find his car keys . . .

Ken would like to thank the following people:

Tom Oliver, who invented the title 'Crime Scene Club' on a tram en route to the Getty Museum, and cooked up the best plots while we sat at his Tiki bar . . . Mr. Levin's Creative Writing students at the Flagstaff Arts and Leadership Academy, *who vetted the books . . . Rob and Jenny Mullen and Victor Viera, my Writer's Group, who shared their lives and invaluable insights . . . My recently deceased father, Dr. A Vern McIntosh, who taught me when I was a child to love written words. This series could not have happened without all of you.*

Series Consultant

Carla Miller Noziglia is Senior Forensic Advisor, Tanzania, East Africa, for the U.S. Department of Justice, International Criminal Investigative Training Assistant Program. A Fellow of the American Academy of Forensic Sciences her work has earned her many honors and commendations, including Distinguished Fellow from the American Academy of Forensic Sciences (2003) and the Paul L.

Kirk Award from the American Academy of Forensic Sciences Criminalistics Section. Ms. Noziglia's publications include *The Real Crime Lab* (coeditor, 2005), *So You Want to be a Forensic Scientist* (coeditor 2003), and contributions to *Drug Facilitated Sexual Assault* (2001), *Convicted by Juries, Exonerated by Science: Case Studies in the Use of DNA* (1996), and the *Journal of Police Science* (1989).

Illustrator

Justin Miller first discovered art while growing up in Gorham, ME. He developed an interest in the intersection between science and art at the University of New Hampshire while studying studio art and archaeology. He applies both degrees in his job at the Public Archaeology Facility at Binghamton University. He also enjoys playing soccer, hiking, and following English Premier League football.